My Mercedes
is Bigger than Yours

NKEM NWANKWO

LONDON
HEINEMANN
IBADAN · NAIROBI · LUSAKA

Heinemann Educational Books Ltd.,
48 Charles Street, London W1X 8AH
P.M.B. 5205, Ibadan · P.O. Box 45314, Nairobi
P.O. Box 3966, Lusaka
EDINBURGH MELBOURNE AUCKLAND TORONTO
HONG KONG SINGAPORE KUALA LUMPUR NEW DELHI

ISBN 0 435 90173 7

First published by Andre Deutsch Limited 1975
First published in African Writers Series 1975

The author wishes to thank Cameron Duodo,
who first thought of the title
My Mercedes is Bigger than Yours,
for allowing him to use it.

Reproduced, printed and bound in Great Britain by
Morrison & Gibb Ltd., London and Edinburgh

PART ONE

The Roots that Clutch

1

Once upon a time a young man was savouring the pleasures of a new car. He was thinking that there were really occasions when a car seemed to drive itself as it were, seemed to respond to some remote stimulus independent of the driver. It had its moments of cursedness, of course, when it whined and snorted for no particular reason, then there were moments of heavenly smoothness when it floated on the crest of some intangible wave.

It was like when you have gone into a woman. Some of the time is taken up with clumsy flopping about; trying futilely to find the perfect position and rhythm. Then there are moments of complete synchronization of limbs which seem to come about without effort. There is then an access of energy and the two bodies seem to fuse into one through some mysterious alchemy of blood. Desire and the explosions of joy in tidal waves originating from impulses as mysterious as they are arbitrary.

In the same way, thought the young man, there are moments of complete physical and emotional accord with a car and these seem to occur more frequently when the car is new. But if he had thought more about it, he would have linked the uneveness of the car's performance with the uneveness of the road. For his country like most countries on the make built roads by fits and starts, always limited by pinched resources. A combination of lean years and greedy road builders who cared more for fat profits than for the comfort of road users, produced ragged death traps in the name of roads while the rarer stretches of smooth tarmac were the fruit of years of opulence.

He would soon be home. Already familiar landmarks were flashing by: occasional clusters of giant trees, the scene of childhood escapades, wooden stores and brothels that stood where once, in his memory, had been wide lawns and friendly trees. Hard-boiled as the young man was, or thought he was, the prospect of the clearing in the forest he knew as home never failed to move him deeply. Involuntarily he broke into a song of praise to home. The song and the exhilaration of spirits and the effortless drive through the balmy twilight almost brought tears to his eyes. He waved to a number of naked children who were grubbing about by the wayside. He failed to notice their nakedness and squalor. He saw them only through the haze of his happiness. My people! My country! he thought. His sense of wellbeing seemed an augury of a happy return.

2

The household of the patriarch, Udemezue Okudo, was astir. The old man had set the pace by rising up much earlier than usual and shouting over the walls of his five wives' huts: "Hoa! Can't you see the sun!" The children were the first to respond to the call as they scrambled to untie the cow which was to be killed in honour of their brother Onuma's return from many years' sojourn in Lagos. Assisted by many willing neighbourly hands, the cow was driven from a nearby grove where it had been browsing, into the Okudo compound and tied to a tree. The children then surrounded and made faces at it. There was a problem now of who was to kill the cow. Cow-killing was a long-established art. And the practitioners were getting fewer and fewer. The old masters were dead. And the young ones who had learned from them had gone into the church.

"Let us send for my brother's son, Nweze. I think he would be at home now," said the first wife, Oliaku.

Udemezue glared at her and grunted. It was a splendid idea though. The boy referred to, Nweze, though a brainless fellow in many ways knew the ritual of cow-killing. But to have to send to a relative a mile away to do a job for one was hard to take. After snuffing angrily for a few moments Udemezue nodded agreement. Oliaku jumped up happily and went to give instructions to a little girl, daughter of one of the younger wives.

"Ada, come here. Go to Mbammili. Tell my brother Okike that my face is full of shame. They know that my son Onuma is coming home today and none of them has done anything." She thought a bit. "Tell them that Udemezue wants them all to come later in the evening."

"Yes mother."

"And tell my brother's son, Nweze, to come now quickly, eh?"

"Yes mother."

The small girl scrambled away but just as she reached the gate the woman shouted: "And listen, Ogoli must not come, do you hear?"

"Yes, mother," said the girl, disappearing through the gate. Oliaku knew that Ogoli would come.

3

Ogoli was another of her nephews in Mbammili. He had especially offended her. She had found a pretty wife for him in Aniocha. But as soon as the bride price was paid he had left off coming to pay his respects to her. He would come to his mother-in-law with presents of fish and game and on his way home carefully make a detour to avoid encountering his aunt.

Udemezue knew what his wife had been at and that this would swell the number of his guests that day. But he didn't mind and went on snuffing placidly.

Relatives were beginning to arrive. The first was predictably Ikenna Ozigbo, popularly known as Magic. He was a tall, lean, squint-eyed man who wore a pair of khaki trousers and a shirt which were washed perhaps once a year. Still, this manner of dressing indicated his awareness of a slight superiority over the villagers. You see, Magic had been abroad to Lagos, Port Harcourt, Kano – by his own accounts. He described himself as an "occult doctor" of all manner of illnesses. He could also make rings and charms to bring success in work and examination to the buyers. He claimed that many influential people – ministers of state, for instance – were his clients.

"What do you think makes men rich? Their cleverness and hard work? Wrong! It is *ogwu*, my friend, powerful *ogwu*, and I can make it for you," Magic would say. Magic was other things besides. He could flute passably on festival occasions. And he was a politician too. Whenever an election was on, he got appointed as an "organising secretary" and could always talk round a large number of the women voters who hadn't the slightest notion of what the issues were. But however useful Magic was as a canvasser he was distrusted. People wouldn't put it beyond him to collect bribe money from both the rival candidates.

4

He breezed into the obi and after a welcome cup of palm wine began at once to recount his latest exploits.

"A strange thing happened at Ubulu, my friends. A man's wife left him. He called me to make him some charm which would bring her back."

"And you did?" asked Udemezue.

"Yes. Two days later she came running back to him. I made a special ogwu. I had to order it from India. This was the first time it was put to use."

"Which Ubulu is this?" said Udemezue.

"On the road to Enugu."

"I know it. About twelve miles to Enugu."

"Ten," said Magic.

"Twelve," asserted Udemezue. He was not going to be contradicted by this young charlatan.

Other members of the umunna were soon drifting in. The last man to come was old Imedu, the oldest member of the family. And it was just as well that the cola had not been broken. He liked to break all the cola in all the kindred households.

"The old bones are getting stiffer and stiffer, children," he said, staggering into the obi.

Magic started up and briskly helped him to his seat. The old man looked fixedly at him.

"Whose son is he?" he asked. It was one of his tricks to pretend not to know people.

"I am the son of Ozigbo," said Magic. "People call me Magic."

"Oh, Magic," said Imedu indifferently. "Magic, did you say?"

"Yes."

"The names you young people have nowadays. Ugh – Magic!" He gingerly tried the seat which was offered to him, didn't seem satisfied with it, but at last slumped into it.

Then he fixed his eyes malevolently on Udemezue. "Udemezue, son of rogues, look at me and see what your fathers have reduced me to. Udemezue, scion of traitors."

Udemezue ignored the taunt. And from the expression of those present it seemed that they were used to the old man's form of address and knew that he meant no harm.

All the same, as he became more decrepit he was increasingly a nuisance. Almost everybody in the village suffered from his tantrums. He was poor and lonely, having lost his wife and all his children, and the villagers had tacitly accepted an obligation to sustain him. They took turns to feed him and clean him up but he seemed to hate most those who helped him. He spent most of his day in the Udemezue household and this made the head of the house an easy target.

Still, few abandoned old Imedu, partly because it was unheard of for the village to abandon an old helpless member and partly because every one understood that his nihilism was a legitimate response to protracted disillusionment and impotence. Imedu at the peak of his youth had been nominated to be the keeper of the village shrine and he had of course to accept. It had been a good job when the religious life of the village revolved round the shrine. But as the ties to the cult which owned the shrine weakened and devotees dropped away, his source of power and living faded. At the end he remained an embarrassing wreckage left by a current which had drifted to new vistas and concerns.

"Udemezue, son of the destroyer of other people's peace—" he choked on a violent curse.

"It is enough, Grandad," said the herdsman, in the tone of one pacifying a child.

6

"Give him the *cola* nut," said Udemezue. "Break *cola* for us, Grandad."

The *cola* nut was passed on to him in a wooden bowl. He broke it, and with a great deal of reluctance distributed the blades, keeping two for himself. Magic served palm wine from a big pot in the middle of the *obi*.

After a second cup of palm wine, the old man knocked the gourd cup on his knees, as if to assure himself that it could break. When he found it intact he looked up with an aggrieved air. "Udemezue Okudo," he rasped.

"What is it, old man?" said Udemezue impatiently.

"Did you say that your son would come back?"

"Yes."

"When?"

"Today. In the evening."

"Well, he won't," shrieked the old man.

"It is well, old man," said Udemezue contemptuously.

"The old man will have his little joke," smiled Magic, "or he may be only drunk."

"Drunk on only one cup of palm wine!" cried Imedu.

"Give him another cup, Ikenna. Shall we give you another cup, Grandad?"

The old man merely snivelled and when the cup was offered to him accepted it roughly. He stood up while drinking and afterwards gazed abstractedly at his seat. "Who gave me this? What a thing to offer an old man!"

Udemezue motioned to Magic and the latter removed the offending seat, a beautifully carved stool, and replaced it with a reclining seat bound with cloth. The old man took this and straight away went to sleep.

The sun was climbing fast and all over the village there were signs and sounds of animated life. It was getting on to the time for the daily market, and neighbours were calling each other up in the elaborate system of bush signalling which they used. From the far fields came the soft wailing of the dove. A little later a singing group was heard moving down the road. The talk then turned on the arrival of Udemezue's son, Onuma.

"He has been away so long. I hope he doesn't find us ignorant villagers strange," said the herdsman.

"I don't trust the young ones," shrieked the old man, waking up. "They desert us when we are old."

The others ignored him.

"They are lucky, these young ones," continued the herdsman. "The world is theirs. They can fly whereever they like. To think that I could have been like them if I had read books. It was during our time that the white man brought books here. But I couldn't read them. I hadn't the patience."

"It takes more than patience to read books," countered somebody amidst laughter.

Udemezue sat aloof. Within, he was tense with expectation of his son's return. It was to be the climax of his career, bigger even than the *ozo*. But outwardly he was calm, almost detached.

"What's keeping that Nweze fellow," he bawled out.

It wasn't long before Nweze, the cow-killer, came. With characteristic ebullience, he began to bawl greetings long before he reached the gate.

"Daughter of our house, we have come."

Oliaku answered: "Welcome, Nweze."

"Come out and tell me what it is all about," Nweze called. He was now standing in front of the *obi*, unabashed before Udemezue's cold stare. Nweze was a giant of a man with an incredibly wide mouth through which issued a rapid flow of words. He was not very

8

clever, but was loved for his large, generous heart and open disposition. He was accompanied by Ogoli.

"Father-in-law, I greet you," said Udemezue.

"Where is our daughter?"

"I am here," said Oliaku, emerging from her hut.

"So your son is coming back, eh? When he was young did I not say he would be a great man? And now, am I not right, oh you young women?" Although Oliaku was old enough to be Nweze's mother he treated her always like a young girl, and she rather liked it.

"Welcome," she said elaborately ignoring Ogoli who stood smiling diffidently behind the giant.

"Shoot the gun and blow the trumpet. It's a day for rejoicing."

"A day for rejoicing indeed," chorused Ogoli.

Oliaku turned furiously on him. "So you came. I thought this house was taboo to you. I thought I was a leper to be avoided."

Small Ogoli smiled broadly. How can you be a leper, daughter?"

"I am," she shouted warming up. "A leper. What are you here for?"

"He is here to see his brother, woman," shouted the men in the *obi*, taking sides with the hard pressed Ogoli. But they needn't have worried, for Ogoli had control of the situation.

"I need no excuse to come here," he said pleasantly. "This is as much my house as any other person's. Where my daughter is, that place is my home."

"Good word," shouted his brother Nweze, shaking the other's hand.

Oliaku didn't want to press the point. She was too elated at the presence of her nephews and at the prospect of her son's return to have much room in her heart to indulge a grudge.

9

"I have nothing more to say," she said and, pretending anger, walked back to her hut.

The newcomers joined those in the obi and exchanged the kind of badinage which was usual on such occasions. They knew one another very well. Mbammili was only a mile away and there was much going to and fro between the two clans.

"Have some palm wine," said Udemezue.

"As if I needed an invitation," said Nweze amidst laughter. "But listen, you mustn't think that I came here only to drink palm wine. I came to welcome my cousin."

"Have some palm wine in any case," laughed Magic.

"Thank you. But one of you ought to taste it first. I can't trust you Aniocha men. You are too clever with charms for my liking."

"Never mind about that," said the herdsman. "If you die your people would be only too pleased to have your body. Delicious." There was a legend that in the days past Mbammili people were cannibals.

"Anyway we are much more practical," bawled Nweze. "We kill and eat. We don't waste human flesh like you scoundrels."

"He has a point there," agreed the herdsman laughing.

The numerous children of the compound had sensed that the long expected cow-killer had come and were sauntering round the obi, constantly finding an excuse to glance idly at their elders. At last, when Nweze had nerved himself with sufficient potations of palm wine, he rose and roared a brisk order. Several hands forced the cow down, tied it up and laid it on a big slaughtering table constructed for the occasion. Nweze with professional smoothness slashed its throat. Then followed the other rituals of burning and carving the huge carcass.

Udemezue had dressed up for his meeting with his son. He wore a long tunic of wool and a cap plumed with parrot's feathers. As he headed for the lorry stop where he was to meet his son, the other members of the *umunna* came with him, all except the old man who still slept.

It was midday now. Streams of people were walking to market. There was a drum group led by the chief drummer of Aniocha, dressed as usual in his wrapper of locally woven broadcloth with the red-striped night-cap on his head. His team comprised four nondescript young men all in various stages of undress. The youngest was only seven years old but already he seemed to have caught the style of the band.

The lorry stop was on the other side of the road from the market.

Udemezue sat in the midst of the waiting group, snuffing interminably and now and then dropping a remark into the general chatter.

The market had not filled up and the quiet of the little town was only now and then broken by some extra noisy lorry that smoked along the highway. It was going to be a long wait. But the *umunna* didn't mind. It was by no means a tedious pastime. They were kept entertained by strings of anecdotes.

The women of the household formed their own little group sitting on their own stools. Some shelled nuts while they waited. But the mother was too nervous to take part in these idle pursuits. She was on a constant lookout for the noise of motor vehicles. Although in her son's letter she had been told that he now had a car, not a lorry, she would constantly jump up whenever a bus or lorry stopped to drop passengers. The waiting group was soon joined by Nweze who had now completed the task of carving.

11

"It was a large cow you had there, Udemezue," he said. "It took almost three hours to carve. You must invite the whole of Aniocha to eat it." He rubbed his hands together and then asked: "Hasn't our friend come?"

"The way is long," said Magic with a knowing gesture.

"How long does the journey take?" asked Nweze.

"It depends," said Magic in a judicial tone. "Lagos can be done in three, sometimes four days."

"I will go there one of these days," said Nweze challengingly. "Mark my words, one of these days I will get to Lagos."

The others laughed. They knew that the ten towns around Aniocha would probably be the limit of Nweze's dream journey.

The sun had become blurred and the evening had taken on its special golden rust colour when the newcomer arrived. A golden coloured Jaguar had jerked to a stop a little way past the waiting group and then slowly, uncertainly backed up to them. A burly, bearded, altogether beautiful youth dressed in an elegant English-made suit emerged from the driver's seat. There was a short doubtful period during which each party failed to recognise the other. Then Oliaku jumped on the stranger and began hugging and kissing him. After the first feverish moments she stood back and surveyed him.

"What's the beard for?" she asked.

"It's old age, mother."

"Well if you are old what will your Father and I be?"

When Onuma had disentangled himself from his mother he shook hands with the other relatives.

"They grow big abroad," roared Nweze, measuring Onuma against his own giant body. "A tiny fellow like that only yesterday, and then *agadam*!" Nweze raised his hands in an eloquent gesture.

As soon as greetings were over, Onuma took charge. "How do we get home? There are too many of us to fit in the car, it seems. Father, you and Mother had better come in. And then. . . ."

"Never mind," said the giant. "I will walk home and so will the rest. There is no hurry. I will take a ride in this car before long. You bet I will. Go ahead, boy. Let your father and mother enjoy the fruit of their sufferings. That's the way it is done. Come along, children," he motioned to the rest of the *umunna*. They rose, beat the dust off their bottoms, and went with him.

Udemezue found himself in a situation well outside his realm of experience. Usually he was the kind of man who liked to be master of his situation. But faced with evidence of his son's affluence he was more stunned than he would have ever thought possible. So he hung back a little and was only prevailed upon to get into the car by the prompting of Magic. Magic had stayed back after the rest of the *umunna* had walked home, ostensibly to chaperon Udemezue and Oliaku, but in reality to take a ride himself. After opening the doors for the parents, he got in himself.

"You see how it is, Mother," said Magic in the tone of a guide.

"I see how it is," replied Oliaku in a tearful voice.

Udemezue was divided between his patriarchal dignity and his sense of triumph at his son's achievements.

A short pathway led from the main road into the big Udemezue compound and Onuma at first hesitated. He was not sure if it would be safe to motor through it. Then he saw a large clearing in front of a neighbour's compound on the other side of the road. He decided to park there. But Udemezue wouldn't hear of it. The clearing belonged to a widow of a retired policeman, a noted gossip who would have placed a construction favourable to her interests on the parking of the car in her yard.

"You have all the parking space you need in my *obi*," he said.

Onuma then carefully, gingerly crunched over the grass-grown pathway, through the large gate with carved doors and into the compound. As soon as the car stopped it was surrounded by the whole family. Passersby, hearing the excited voices, came to know what it was about and stayed to admire the car.

Long before Onuma was due to come home Udemezue had been planning a reception. By far the most troublesome problem was building a house worthy of the young man. There was an empty mud grass-thatched house which the children had used when they were young. Udemezue didn't think it would be good enough for Onuma. Something more in keeping with his new status was required. So Udemezue had built a small house of cement blocks roofed with corrugated iron. It was hard to raise the money. But just as he was starting to build the house one of the girls had been married and being fairly pretty her bride price was quite substantial. This, added to money obtained from a few other transactions such as the sale of part of the yam holdings, enabled him to build a comfortable two-room house. There it stood, new, smart and isolated from all the other mud grass-roofed homes in the compound. Udemezue suggested taking Onuma straight there but the latter said no.

"I must first sit in the old *obi*. Haven't seen it for ages. Take my things to the other house," he ordered the children.

14

Udemezue acquiesced with some inward reservation. The young fellow was a little too peremptory.

Old Imedu was still sleeping in the *obi*. As soon as the company arrived he jumped up and peered beadily at Onuma.

"Do you know me, son?"

"Yes," said Onuma. "You are the shrine-keeper. You keep the shrine."

"Kept," said the old man with a dry cackle and at the same time walking out. "Now it is the shrine that keeps me."

Nweze wanted to hear all the news of Lagos. He was especially curious about the car. To his simple mind it seemed incredible that one who was so small only a few years ago could now own a car.

"My son," this was a favourite expression of his, "My son, what is it you do?"

Onuma smiled. His profession, that of public relations promoter, bore no relation to any form of experience Nweze would have had, and so he had no language to describe it to him. Instead he adopted his own favourite method of evading difficult questions. He romanticized. He described himself as a traveller, a sampler of exotic cultures. There was the time he led a wild convoy of cars for thousands of miles. Then he had been the first non-believer to visit the harem of a sultan. He drew a vivid picture of groundnut pyramids that "reach the sky" and capped the story with tales of wild horse rides on the plains of the Sudan.

He talked with extravagant gestures and his brown brilliant eyes took in everybody challengingly. The peasants drank in the story. At the end Nweze asked with mock envy: "My son, how does one become a good traveller? Does one need to have read books or what?"

"All you need is a spirit of adventure. The will to dare. In the middle ages. . . ."

"Middle ages, my son?"

"In ancient times men had that spirit. White men all had the spirit of adventure."

"Spirit of adventure," mused Nweze. "Try me."

When it appeared that the subject was exhausted Onuma rose and retired to his house. But his father's party continued far into the night.

3

Alone, Onuma felt the elation of arrival fade away and a heavy depression began to weigh down his spirits. There was so much about the village that dampened one's spirits. There was the sudden darkness for instance. His room was lighted by a miniature oil lamp made of an empty cigarette tin in which a wick had been stuck. It shed a sickly light that only accentuated the heavy brooding darkness. Onuma had never liked the darkness. He was by nature a child of bright lights.

The villagers had gone to bed already. They slept like animals, with the dusk. In Lagos Onuma would just have been getting ready for one of his numerous night prowls, washing, scenting himself, selecting the most tantalizing ties to go with one of his dozens of suits. He had brought a large number of his elegant clothes with him, but knew he would have no occasion to use them. Besides, it was such a big risk airing any of his expensive things at home. That was perhaps the most off-putting aspect of the place, its dirtiness and a general tendency for anything that came in contact with it to become soiled.

Talk about the simple life! The main attraction to this kind of life was supposed to be its simplicity and uncomplicatedness. Those who admired the simple life, always of course, from the comfortable distance of urban conveniences, never took into account its squalor. As for the simple-life livers, the peasants, who were supposed to be so vital, Onuma now remembered that he knew better. The peasant was only too likely to be dirty, drunken and superstitious.

Onuma, of course, was himself born and bred in the village, although because of his father's relative wealth he had never really known manual work. His outlook manifested itself in his easy assumption that the world existed to minister to his fulfilment. A beautiful body and ease of manner had enabled him to sustain his attitude without too much strain. He instinctively sought people and things that were fulfilled and saved, people rich in mind and body. He had very little patience with the other types. He despised weakness and folly. He hated sick people, small people, mean people, ugly people.

Onuma conceived of himself as a man of the Renaissance whose spiritual ancestors came from among the Medicis. He had never needed to assert himself because he saw from experience that the world accepted him.

Even when he attended elementary school in his home village, his escapades and brilliance were a legend in the whole district. He was later taken up by a wealthy uncle, a businessman in the city, and sent to a most exclusive school. The effect of the exclusiveness was to confirm him in the notion that he was better than the next man. For the school, a sort of half-baked Eton with an "old boy" network and other canned myths, specialized in taking a varied assortment of boys – peasants, parvenue children, sons of illiterate but

17

moneyed politicians, offspring of poverty-stricken slums
– nourishing their egotism, and teaching them conceit
and disdain for the lives they would be called upon to
lead. Onuma seemed to escape damage because his circumstances and his personality shielded him against
disillusionment. Others fared worse and developed a
world view which, bearing not even the remotest relationship to reality, arrested their development forever.

Onuma enjoyed school enormously. He found work
easy. Besides, hard work, referred to contemptuously as
"swotting", was rather looked down upon. The battle
of life was to be won on the playing fields, not in a
science laboratory. Application or swotting was something for the maimed and the incomplete, the small
rugged-featured boys, who wore specs and didn't see too
well. The boys who counted, who wore decent clothes and
played decent soccer, could always get by without it. In
spite of his attitude to work, he got on very well with
the masters, mostly easy-going, sleepy men who affected an ironic attitude to their profession. At first one or
two of them invited him to drinks and made passes at
him, but he didn't take offence because basically he despised and patronised teachers as a class.

With the boys he was enormously popular. He had
a charismatic effect on them as a crowd. Whenever he
approached any gathering they always raised a loud
ovation.

The only disappointment of his school career was that
toward the end he failed to be made a prefect. The boys
were scandalized at first, but finally accepted the result.
After all, they reasoned, being made a prefect would
have dented their hero's image, limiting his role as the
uncommitted princeling, the arbiter of taste, and giving
him the more dubious role of disciplinarian. As for
Onuma, the effect of the disappointment was to de-

velop in him a streak of dislike for authority. He formed a habit of devising various means of outwitting it.

It was at this stage that he discovered all the vices. He formed a small group of rakes who made frequent midnight incursions into the Lagos brothels. He was also beginning to discover his power over women. They couldn't, they said, resist his large, warm, mischievous eyes. His face, too, intrigued them. One of his Lagos women swore that if you watched Onuma for a full minute you would note about five different expressions playing about in his face. And he seemed to produce them unconsciously.

As he matured and improved his methods women spoilt him, threw themselves at him. Instead of mellowing him, this caused Onuma to develop a style of self-protective brutality to women. But this they loved even more.

The transition from school to university was inevitable. The country had just built its first university, the most expensive of status symbols. About a third of the country's annual resources had gone into the construction. There it stood, a brilliant spectacle of glass and tiles in the midst of the mud-cracked slums of the native city. The first students were few and enjoyed all the privileges of rarity. The country made much of them, denied them nothing.

Being one of a handful of students to receive a university education in a country of millions did not improve Onuma's or any of the students' humility.

But in some ways the university was for Onuma an anticlimax. It seemed to be mostly a repetition of most of the things he had done in school. He never experienced the exhilaration of freedom which boys are supposed to feel on first entering a university. Because of the curious arrangement by which the university year in Nigeria began at the end of everybody else's year, he had nine months to kill after leaving school. He had taken a well paid job, rented a flat, organized all-night orgies, savoured the pleasures of sleeping with girls in his very own apartment.

In the university he was brought up sharp by the new concept of work. At school his teachers had taken his potential brilliance for granted and had let him off lightly. As a result he had developed the habit of wide but unsystematized reading. The university teachers were ruthless in their insistence on regular systematic reading. They all liked him. He had a presence, unlike the rather scrofulous crowd they received yearly, but they had seen many like him before too, young men of sparkle and dash who frittered away their talents and energy and in the end came to nothing.

To Onuma it only seemed that the lecturers were determined to prove to him that he was not as clever as he thought he was. But of course he had never thought himself "clever" in the academic sense. He did not seek a good degree. Doing so would have involved competing with the scrofulous crowd and he couldn't bring himself that low. Neither was he a scholar. He knew the type, dour young men with piles of books sticking out of their weird bicycles, and he enjoyed having fun at their expense. After years of cruel brainwashing, they would end up in some safe academic hole, the very little originality, the talent, individuality and imagination they had started off with would be buried under a load of other people's ideas and opinions which they took to be learning.

Surely there must be a way by which with the application of minimal effort he could obtain some sort of certificate. The word "certificate" was then a magic password in Nigerian society, a highly priced bill of exchange. What one did to obtain it was immaterial. In any case, the information one crammed into one's head would be forgotten a few days after examination day and was mostly useless. What was the sense in observing the eccentricities of English phonemes, or following the history of the decline and fall of Anglo-Saxon rounded and unrounded vowels in stressed and unstressed positions? And what had Spencer's cloying luxury to say to a person brought up on the stark realities of a poverty-stricken, arid land?

Meanwhile Onuma was learning the kind of thing which to him mattered. He was already a personality in the university's rudimentary drama school. He became a connoisseur of wines and cigars. He was on first name terms with the keepers of all the brothels and pubs in town. He was observing life in the raw and every day he felt that he was learning more and more about the two most powerful forces of life, sex and money. He had a theory that if a man knew how to control money and sex he didn't need to learn anything else. In fact Onuma did learn a little about sex, but as for money, he would never learn how to deal with it. True to the bohemian tradition, he despised money and flung it away carelessly whenever he got hold of it.

By the time of his second year at the university, his code of life was set. It was a code of complete, unashamed individualism. The only obligation the individual owed was to his own fulfilment. The rest of the world could and should look after itself. The individual must try to fulfil himself emotionally and physically, to the best of his ability, short of getting into trouble with the law.

However it was also a fact of life that self-enhancement was impossible without the cooperation of other people. To obtain a certificate, the password to the good life, Onuma had to maintain some semblance of work, to cultivate his teachers. The latter came in all sorts. There were a handful of good men who combined fine scholarship with originality of mind and refined urbanity. One had only reverence for these people. Then of course there were the usual dregs of the English academic world who sought a niche in the less demanding atmosphere of a new world. One couldn't have much to do with them, particularly as their basic insecurity forced them to erect a barrier between themselves and their students. The university staff also included some Nigerians, sad figures who, beaten down, prevented from having any say in the government of a white-dominated university in their own country, would seem to have lost confidence in themselves and to have accepted their inferiority. The less said about these the better. Onuma's sympathy warmed to the younger English dons who came over to Nigeria for a year or two and whose idealism and integrity was not yet beaten out by years of intractable university racial, tribal and academic battles.

Onuma struck up a warm friendship with one of them. His name was Brian, a brilliant fellow who had just taken a double first from Oxford and had come down with a year's fellowship to Nigeria. He was very much excited about Nigeria which he saw as possessing the possibilities for ethical growth which England and the older industrial nations had not taken advantage of in their advance toward materialism. The older countries had failed. His favourite expression was "Europe is finished", by which he meant not that it was physically or even economically broken, but that it was spiritually bankrupt. Africa was virgin land, a *tabula rasa* on which much that is pure could be written. Africans would learn from the mistakes of the older nations and have the opportunity to forge a just society. Onuma was very fond of Brian, although he thought his idealism a little naive. He decided he would show him what Africa, this potential Utopia, was really like. He introduced Brian to all the brothels in town and there were many evenings when they engaged in arguments about commitment and non-attachment while, nearby, prostitutes haggled with prospective clients.

Among the students Onuma had few friends. He was always pained by the immaturity and roughness of the majority of the students. Instead he identified with a small minority of handsome easy-going loafers. Apart from giving conscientious teachers stomach ulcers they had one more thing in common, a feeling that they had seen through the academic racket and were determined not to be taken in. Some of these fire-raisers were later to form the nucleus of a social and political upheaval in their country.

Maintaining a semblance of work was not as easy as it sounded. Onuma found his capacity for steady application, never very remarkable, taxed to the limit. Finally, towards the end of his academic career when his mates were sweating in anticipation of the exams and hard-bitten teachers were licking their lips in anticipation of the rude remarks they were going to make on his examination paper ("No!"; "Wrong!"; "Nonsense!"; "Hello, what's this?"; "Terrible!") he threw up his career and quit.

The other hard-pressed students were at first inclined to smile knowingly at the news that their Prince Marlowe was funking his exams, but their smiles faded when they heard that Onuma had captured a job which would pay him twice as much money as any student could reasonably expect after graduation. For a few days after that one heard from the final year students nothing but criticisms of the academic calling and its niggardly financial rewards. One or two delinquent characters actually followed Onuma's example, though lacking his gifts they came to disaster.

Onuma worked as a public relations official for a European firm based in Lagos. With his good looks and charm his employers found him a natural for the job. His main task was to ease the social forms between corrupt Nigerian politicians and civil servants and the European businessmen who corrupted them. There were occasions, too, when London-based managers visited Nigeria and took time off to sample the salacious pleasures which the capital city offered. Onuma put his unmatched knowledge of city haunts at their disposal. He was a combination of go-between, con-man and pimp. He enjoyed these roles enormously. Six months after he got the job he applied for and obtained a loan to buy a car. At first he was made to put his name to far more papers than he could afford to remember. Then, towards the end of the negotiation, he was called in to see the General Manager of the firm, Mr Karolides.

"I see you want to buy a Jaguar," Mr Karolides began.

"Yes," said Onuma firmly.

Mr Karolides blinked up at him in mild puzzlement. He was a broad-faced, white-haired, distinguished looking man. "Why, if I may ask?" he asked with a little stammer.

Oh for a movie camera, mused Onuma. The question could only be answered beautifully in a film sequence with a series of flashbacks. First: a scene engraved on Onuma's impressionable mind. *Dramatis personae*: he, Onuma, and a girl of luscious sexual power. Let the camera play on his face, confident and trusting in the goodness of the female heart. Then let the camera glance down to his feet to scrutinize his gait a little nervous but stiffening for a life-and-death test of manhood. Then move on to the girl and do a good job there, please. Feed the viewer's lust with a riot of images. Then cut to a scene touched with not too much halo. Boy meets girl with a promise of happiness ever after. Let this idyll be disturbed by the intrusion of a satyr in a high powered car who, aided by the car, worsts Hyperion. It would not be difficult after that to hint at an Orphean resolve by Hyperion to descend to the nether world, if need be, to rescue his ravished ego. Next, cut to Lagos street scenes with selective shots of status cars. All makes are represented here as everyone can see. The Jag, for obvious reasons, is rare.

The script next calls for some Freudian comment on the competitiveness of Hyperion's temper: how he always went for the top prize in everything and if he failed to get it something died in him.

"Do you realize that well over half of your salary would go into instalmental payments on a Jaguar?" asked Karolides.

"I know," smiled Onuma. Marvellous fellow, the manager. Cautious, prudent, far-sighted, well insured. Loyal husband and loving father, no doubt. What would he know about the type of character who lived only for spectacular moments? One of Onuma's friends had saved up money for most of his life. Then he had thrown it into the first instalment (about a third of the cost) of a sports model. He drove the superb vehicle for a month and when he couldn't pay the second instalment the firm took the car away from him. But the youth was unperturbed. As far as he was concerned it was enough to have driven the princely car for a month. The experience compensated for his enormous loss.

"Well, you can smile now," said Mr Karolides.

"When we begin to deduct you will do the other thing."
He signed the last paper which authorized a money-lending firm to lend money to Onuma at a rapacious rate of interest and on the guarantee of the firm.

The buying of the Jaguar completed the making of a romantic egotist. And Onuma came home to celebrate.

4

Onuma's mother's hut was the one place in the village which was exempt from his censure. There couldn't be anything wrong with it. It contained too many tender memories cemented by love of the ageing woman who was briskly cooking. She seemed never to tire, even in her old age.

"You know Mother, I have been away for fifteen years."

"It is long," said Oliaku, bustling to her cooking.

"You haven't changed. You are still a young girl," he continued.

"Young girl, indeed," laughed Oliaku. "Now, mind your clothes. You shouldn't be sitting on the ground."

"Never mind, mother."

Onuma had escaped from the new iron-roofed house with its creaking iron bed into his mother's hut, and sat on the raised mud bed that ran round the building. This was the place which in his mind's eye had always represented home. There was the well-known and well-loved living room with its three raised earth beds that served for seats, the fireplace with a built-in mud shelf and the sheaf of maize suspended from the grass-thatched roof. Although he hadn't seen it for fifteen years it was as familiar as the palm of his hand. So was the bitter-leaf soup that his mother cooked for him. She remembered that this was his favourite dish and must have gone to considerable trouble to prepare it. He knew how she would value his compliments and so was lavish with them.

"Mother, this is the best bitter-leaf soup I have ever tasted."

"Is it so?" She was like a young girl complimented on her looks.

As he ate, she sat and watched him, completely at peace and fulfilled in him. At the end of the meal he endeavoured to interest her in his activities but her answers showed that she wasn't very much interested. So he dozed fitfully, every now and then waking up to glance at the silent woman and the peaceful circle created by the palm oil light.

5

Onuma woke in a room depressingly bare of furniture. It was the third day of his stay in Aniocha. The room was such a sharp contrast from the one he had slept in the night before the last that he felt displaced. He found it difficult to organize anything for the day. First he needed a wash. Then he remembered the rudimentary arrangements made for washing. A small space at the back of the yard had been fenced in with bamboo and palm leaves. A bucket of water would be taken there. Then, standing on the wet soil, one sloshed water all over one's body. Onuma would rather not bathe, at least for the day.

From the rough concrete verandah in front of his

house he could see the *obi* filling with people. Very soon they would be asking for him. So he hastened to put on one of his less expensive but elegant dressing gowns, and sauntered to the *obi*. Udemezue, flanked by Magic, was sitting in the midst of several uncouth looking, brawny men.

"These are the work fellows." Udemezue waved a careless hand towards the men who were about twenty in number. Most were dressed in loincloths and a few in tattered shorts. They sat or squatted on the raised mud bed that ran around the *obi* and gazed at Udemezue with sheepish eyes. They were labourers recruited from a depressed area of the country. They usually took up residence with a well-to-do family in Aniocha and paid their rent in the form of so many days work on the farm weekly. For the other days they hired themselves out to other Aniocha men for some fixed daily payment. Udemezue had employed a large number of them for a farming season and paid them by the month, but after the first two months he had stopped their payment. The labourers had continued working for many more months. At the end of the season, during the harvest, they had demanded their back pay but Udemezue had given each of them a number of yams with the remark: "Money is all very well but you want to start your own farms and with the price of yams being what it is, how much can money buy for you?" The labourers, intimidated, had taken the yams and as soon as they were out of earshot virulently cursed their employer.

A new planting season was to start after the first yam festival and Udemezue had called them again to brief them.

"You all know the farms you farmed for me. You are each to return there. Next week you receive seed yams and I shall come round as usual to watch. We want more care taken of the farms this time, of course."

The men sat glum, demurring. At last somebody who seemed to be their leader hinted that they couldn't feel sure of the terms of the contract.

"Terms?" said Udemezue. "What terms?" He looked sideways at Magic and Onuma. He liked to have sympathetic people beside him when he carried out such delicate bargains. Magic took the cue and laughed.

"What terms?" Udemezue asked with a frown.

"Money!" roared the leader of the labourers, seemingly exasperated beyond his patience. "Are we to be paid money or not? Our wives and children are suffering and the price of things is rising. We have had enough!"

Udemezue waited for him to make an end with the ironical expression of one humouring a child. At last, when the labourer had ended with an incoherent mutter he said in a gentle, contemptuous tone: "Did I say I would not pay you. Why do you create trouble for yourself?"

"It is not that, master," said another of the labourers, attempting to conciliate Udemezue. "It is only that times have been hard, very hard! I must not tell you a lie."

"You do good work," answered Udemezue, "and leave the rest to me. You will get your due."

The labourers rose and shambled out, muttering among themselves.

Udemezue was pleased at the outcome of the palaver. He had not needed to browbeat them. They knew he had the whip hand; if they refused to work they would be run out of town back to their famine districts.

"The fools!" laughed Magic. "It is like them to think

29

of reward first when they should be thinking about the work they should do to earn it."

Onuma had admired and been in close sympathy with his father's dealing with the peasants, though left to himself, he would probably have driven them harder.

"How do you like your house?" asked Udemezue.

Onuma saw that the old man was fishing for a compliment and said: "Oh, it's new and good."

"But nothing compared to what you have in Lagos," laughed Magic.

"Oh, houses are all the same. Just as long as one finds somewhere to shelter from the rain and the sun," Onuma lied.

Udemezue was hardly satisfied with this but snuffed placidly for a while.

Onuma saw he had upset the old man and in order to mollify him, he asked him what arrangements were being made for the big feast to celebrate his return.

Udemezue was pleased but didn't let it show for the sake of his dignity.

The feast was to take place the next Sunday, in three days' time, and according to Udemezue it was to be the greatest thing that ever happened to the district. The feast was to last five days. They were going to offer a cow on each separate day, and many goats and chickens. Most of the women of Aniocha were already baking cassava, and the palm wine tappers had standing orders.

"Anyway," said Udemezue, "I have run out of money and you have to help me."

All the money, of course, was coming from Onuma but it was good to preserve the fiction that it was the old man's feast.

That Sunday morning Onuma was awakened by his little brother, Philip, a thin big-eyed lad of ten who was looked upon as the potential scholar of the family.

"Good morning, sir," the boy said in English. Onuma replied in Ibo: "Oh, Philip how are you, you slept well?"

"Father is coming to church," the boy said excitedly.

"So I heard." Onuma yawned, still tired. "Could you polish my shoes for me, Philip?"

"Yes, sir," While Philip worked he kept up a steady stream of chatter. He felt an intense pleasure at working for this legendary big brother of his.

"The Reverend Father doesn't live here. He lives in Isu, but he comes every other Sunday to say Mass. Today is our own day. And I am going to serve in Mass. I know all the words of the Mass."

"Give me some of them," Onuma challenged him.

"Very well, listen." He stopped polishing to concentrate. *"Credo in unum Deum, Patrem ominpotentem, factorem caeli et terra, visibilium omnium, et invisibilium."*

"What does all that mean?" Onuma challenged him. "Say it in English."

"They are just the words of the Mass. You have to learn them."

"Can you say the 'I believe in God'?" Onuma asked.

"I believe in God the Father almighty, creator of Heaven and earth."

"That's what the words of the Mass mean. Haven't they told you that?"

"No."

"Well, you ought to go and talk to the parish priest."

Philip burst into derisive laughter. Apparently he considered braving the parish priest the ultimate in daring.

He had done a passable job with the shoes and now waited for further instructions. "You want to have your bath?" he asked.

"Yes."

"I will show you. We have a new bathroom for you."
The boy fetched water in a bucket and took it to the
bamboo bathroom and then waited chattering through
the closed door while Onuma washed.

Onuma, after getting dressed, went to check up on
the car. He found his mother waiting by it dressed in the
colourful *buba* and wrapper he had sent her a few months
before. Onuma settled her in the back seat and then
went to call his father.

Udemezue surprised everybody by the glee with
which he looked forward to church going. He hadn't
become a Christian yet, but going into the church to put
up a show before those cocky church people appealed
to his lordly temper. When Onuma arrived at the *obi*
he was busy cleaning up many tokens of the *ozo*, which
he hadn't worn for some time.

A face bobbed out from an opening in the grass ceiling at the top of the *obi*. It was Magic's.

Since Onuma's return Magic had assumed the role of
factotum to the Udemezue household. He had just
mounted a ladder to bring down an *ozala* which was
stuck on the rafters of the *obi*. The huge elephant tusk
was slowly lowered and laid beside the family gods, all
gnarled with age.

Soon Udemezue emerged from the *obi* preceded by
Magic, bearing the family ceremonial *ozala*, or ivory.
It proved a hard job to find a place for it in the car. At
first they tried the boot but this wasn't big enough. But
Magic, by astute juggling, was able to lodge the tusk on
the floor of the car below the front seats.

Udemezue was settled at the back of the car. Magic
discreetly climbed in beside the driver. But just as they
were starting Onuma noticed Philip gazing at them
with his big eyes. "Come and take a ride, Philip," he said.

"No, let him walk," ordered Udemezue. "Go on boy, follow your brothers."

But Onuma could not get away from those big wistful eyes. "He can stay with me here in front. Come along, Philip."

And lastly the ozo staff had to be accommodated. Udemezue held it horizontally, its point towards the dashboard. But this position was inconvenient and could not be maintained, especially when small Philip took up further space on the front seats. So the spear had to be positioned lengthwise and its brass top pushed out the back window. In this position it remained throughout the journey, an object of wonder to bystanders and a menace to pedestrians and cyclists.

The golden Jaguar made quite a stir as it drew up. It was not the only car parked in the front of the small church but it was the only new one. The others were ancient species belonging to merchants who had come from the nearby towns to spend the weekend in Aniocha. The church congregation had settled in their seats and the priest was expected any moment.

Just before the family went into the church, Oliaku whispered something into the ear of her son. Magic with attentive adroitness caught the message and nodded his head vigorously as if in approval of what she said.

"What is it?" asked Udemezue.

"Oh, the church fees," said Onuma. He handed Magic some money and the latter walked importantly into the church. A little later the catechist, a tubby figure with a smooth shining head, emerged with happy eyes and unctuous manner.

"Well, praises to God and the Blessed Virgin. Chief Udemezue has seen the light at last. Welcome." He shook hands with Onuma but lost interest in him at once and concentrated on the father. At first he found the *ozo* tokens hard to take. Both the staff which Udemezue carried and the *ozala* were symbols with slight overtones of paganism, but the catechist decided it would be unwise now to split hairs.

Udemezue accepted the catechist's attention without comment. He remembered the many efforts that had been made by various sects to convert him and he had always treated these attempts with deep contempt.

All the benches in the little church had been taken and to accommodate the newcomers the catechist had to clear a whole bench, to the fury of a rising young taxi-driver who was in the same age group as Onuma and felt hurt at the latter being preferred to him. Another place had to be found for him further back in the church and there he formed a highly vocal centre of discontent for the rest of the service.

Perhaps because of the unaccustomed presence of one of the leaders of the village, the catechist exerted himself more than usual. Normally his authority was undoubted. He usually overshadowed the performance of the officiating white priest by his patent energy. On this day his presence was ubiquitous. He hushed noise-makers all down the aisle. He settled quarrels over the ownership of seats. He took over the choir from a school teacher and bawled over the voices of the young choristers. When the time came for the sermon he interpreted the priest's message in Ibo, simplifying his abstruse dogma and putting in a strong word or two for his pet theories and against his pet enemies. When the Reverend Father had gone, the catechist settled down to his own preaching and made quite a long job of it. Finally he announced that he had the authority of the priest to say that the day's Mass was being said to the glory of God and in grateful thanks to him for returning safely home "our brother, the son of Chief Udemezue Okudo", and making the Chief himself see the light.

At the end of the Mass, Onuma and his father were taken to see the church leaders. Magic came too, hovering in the background and missing no chances.

The most prominent of the church leaders was a man known generally as Tailor, this being his trade. He was a tall, thin stern-faced individual with bristling whiskers. Onuma remembered that when he was young, Tailor had terrorized the children by his ferocity. He was a bogeyman to malingerers. If you missed a catechism class or did not attend a Saturday communal work, Tailor would get to know about it. And he had no scruples about using the whip though he had no specific authority to do so.

Tailor had mellowed with age. Onuma seemed to catch him now and then trying to tip him what looked very much like a sly wink. And when it came to the plaudits for the one who had made good, he gave more than most.

The catechist had decided that he had publicised the Okudo family enough and would now let the other leaders indulge their love of talk. Tailor took up one of Onuma's former teachers on his claim that the foundation of Onuma's fame had been laid by teachers.

"What about us who kept this church going for twenty years? Without a church, could you have had schools, and without schools where would teachers be?"

The teacher saw the fallacy of Tailor's argument but was too dignified to contest the point and left the older man to imagine he had carried the argument.

Udemezue sat silently throughout the palaver. He would have felt impatient except that he accepted the occasion as a tribute to Onuma. But as for the younger man, to sit and hear these older men who had intimidated him in childhood now extolling him rather went to his head, and in a moment of exaltation he rose and volunteered the sum of fifty pounds to the church fund. The effect of his speech was electric. The church leaders rose in uproar, embracing, shaking hands and slapping each other on the back and the atmosphere around the car as the visitors moved to it was near that of a riot. Before it subsided, Magic and Tailor had begun competing for places in the car.

"Have you ever been in a car?" asked Magic.

"When did you become an Okudo man?" bawled Tailor ferociously.

"If you step into this car, I'll— I don't know what I'll do, I swear. . . . ."

"Ha ha!"

Onuma settled the matter by letting both of them come with him, one in front and the other making a third with his parents in the back. But for a while they continued to glare at each other until the comforts of the car presumably dispelled their choler.

A large crowd was waiting at home. The *obi* was filled and the people were spread out under the shading trees of the compound. They were mostly *umunna* men and relatives from the other villages, come for the feast of the cow. As soon as Udemezue sat down women in relays brought hunks of the beast to him. There were certain limbs of the cow which belonged by custom to specific elders in the *umunna*. Udemezue had to make sure that these parts were intact. The carver himself, Nweze, bustling about, was there as an authority to advise him. Udemezue cared little for his peers in the kindred group but he was going to make certain that they all got their due. Old Imedu had his own portion and cursed Udemezue roundly for it. But one member of the Okudo family seemed exempt from the old man's hatred, Oliaku, the chief wife. She had come in from outside and was passing by the *obi* when the old man called out: "Mother, do we have good bitter-leaf at home?"

"We do our best," she replied with a slight laugh.

"Good woman. You are not of these rogues. Udemezue Okudo, I spit in your face." And with that he buried his scanty teeth in a hunk of cow flesh.

Magic was very busy serving palm wine, paying off palm wine tappers who had brought their calabashes to the compound and keeping cuts for himself.

Onuma had taken a number of the young guests to his room. One of them was the "revolutionary", the rising taxi-driver who had been driven from his seat in the church. His name was Chukwuemeka, shortened to Chuks in accordance with the latest fashion. He had now mellowed with some glasses of beer and teased Onuma: "I used to beat you."

"When did you beat me?" Onuma made a mock lunge at the taxi-driver.

"Is he denying it? I will beat him again."

"Go and fight with people in your age group."

With companions of his age, Onuma could now put up his feet. They were crude fellows but they had energy and could make Onuma laugh. "Tell us about Lagos girls," the taxi-driver said.

"Those girls are gorgeous and you can have them for almost nothing. And they can do the thing very well."

This was followed by a great deal of coarse laughter.

There was a slight commotion close to the *obi*. And a woman's voice was heard shouting: "They told me nothing about it. But I got to hear. Nobody is going to hide anything from me."

A tall beautiful woman was standing full-blown in

37

the compound, her eyes fixed accusingly on Udemezue. It was his sister Chijiokie who had been married out to the next town. All the men stirred and smiled at her respectfully.

"Welcome, daughter," they said ingratiatingly.

She ignored them and addressed her brother. "Where is my son, our son if you like." Udemezue slowly pointed to the iron house.

"So that's where you have hidden him?" She strode to Onuma's house calling out, "Come out, young man." Onuma emerged tipsily.

"Go on, bend over," she ordered.

He inclined his body slightly. She patted him on the back. "See how big the small boy has grown. Now where is my own share of the meat?" He went into the house and returned with some velveteen cloth.

"Look at my prize, you skinflints," she shouted, showing the cloth. "You can't prevent me from being lucky, can you?" She danced about for a while amidst general applause, then joined the men in the obi and out-talked them all.

The umunna was complete. In a short time the rest of Aniocha would be coming for the feast.

The high point of the celebration was to be a ceremony of libation to the car.

The Jaguar had been brought near the obi. There it squatted in regal repose like a giant totem, festooned with ritual flowers. All the family were now beginning to compose themselves to a mood of solemnity when they were interrupted by old Imedu, who staggering up, pointed dramatically at Onuma. "He is my son," he shrieked.

"Yes, of course he is your son," said Onuma's mother, trying to calm the old man.

The interruption only made Imedu more violent.

"He is to come after me, do you hear," he cried still pointing at Onuma. "He is now the priest of the shrine, the Lord of the festival, the health of the harvest, the freshener of the waters. My son is lord of the festival and the freshener of the waters. Will you bow to the priest of the shrine?" he barked.

"Enough of that, old man," said Magic impatiently.

"And you!" cried Imedu turning viciously on Magic, "You son of an empty father, you bastard from a mongrel clan. Do you dare to stop me when I give my *ofo* to my successor."

"Leave the old man alone," said somebody.

"Let him come out," shouted Imedu holding the crowd with staring hypnotic eyes. "Let him tangle with the priest of the shrine." And as nobody interrupted he went on. "I am already dead. My spirit went out with the cry of the owl last night and came up in the sky this morning in colours of the rainbow. But my son lives. I am tired, but he lives. My son is priest of the shrine and you must bow to him."

The last bit of the speech was in the form of a tired mumble as the old man slumped into an empty seat.

The rest of the ceremony fell flat after this drama. First there was the pouring of the libation with a "hot drink". There was general agreement that a "hot drink" – whisky, brandy, schnapps or gin – would be more potent than palm wine for the libation. "The car," said Magic "cannot drink palm wine. Palm wine is too far below its dignity." Then came a series of speeches when various clansmen in varying degrees of sobriety extolled the luck of the clan in possessing the mythical car.

"From today," said the herdsman, "we are the greatest. Any clan which claims they are equal with us, let them come out!"

The speech received applause.

"I am going home," old Imedu announced after the applause. "You fellows can all eat shit." He spat hard out into the air. "I am the priest of the shrine. And if Udemezue says no, let him eat shit!"

6

The feast was over. Hundreds of people from the five towns had been there and carried home cow meat and praises for the Udemezue name. In the compound the numerous young men hired to serve had sweated and had made peace between rival clans who fought over privileges connected with special limbs of the cow.

Onuma was relieved. A few days later he thought he would make the rounds of the village. His mother had urged him to go round and cultivate the neighbours. It was the kind of manorial job that he did not very much fancy. But his mother had been persistent and to please her he went. He had not had a good look at the town and now that he did so he was astonished at how fast it was deteriorating. Most of the houses were tumbling down and nobody seemed to care to rebuild them. Perhaps it was the dry season that added to the strangely naked look of the landscape. Many of the huge iroko trees had shed their leaves and a number of plots had been burnt. The people had a mournful look and appeared as if they could do with some nourishment. They were mostly old men and small children. The younger people had all left for the towns. Onuma found it hard in a vague sort of way to reconcile this ghost town with the lush places of his youth.

It was difficult to drive over the pathways in the village for they were now overgrown with weeds. Every Christmas the young men returned from the towns and rebuilt the roads, but as soon as they turned their backs the bush reasserted its sway.

Onuma first visited the house of a rich man called Dilibe for no better reason than that the approaches to it were clearest. The ozo was not in but the women and children were very glad to see him. The first wife he visited, a very fat coal-black individual, gave the others a signal. They all ran to her hut exclaiming: "What have you brought us from Lagos?"

"I came to drink your bitter-leaf soup," he said.

They laughed and teased him more. He riposted, played with the children and then left.

Well, it had been a success after all. He sighed with relief. The only hitch was that the women would expose their obscene-looking breasts. He knew of nothing uglier than a flat, tired breast hanging limply down a village woman's chest.

As he was coming out from another of his visits he saw somebody leaning familiarly against the car. It was Magic.

"You are rolling around?" he asked Onuma with a smile.

"Yes," Onuma replied brusquely getting into the car. But Magic with a pleasant manner and a firm grip, detained him.

"This is between you and me," he said conspiratorially. "I haven't spoken to your father about this because I wasn't quite sure that he would understand. Their ways are, you understand, old-fashioned."

Onuma was getting impatient but Magic took his time in unfolding his story.

"What I was coming to is this: have you some protection?"

41

"What do you mean by protection?"

"You must be protected against accidents, and against the ill-will of your enemies. The world is bad nowadays. No man thinks any good of his fellows. And unless you are protected they will get you."

"I have all the protection I need," said Onuma squaring his bulky shoulders.

"Yes, you may be able to deal with the things you can see but what about the things that come on you unawares. How can you defend yourself against the Evil Eye. Tell me that?"

"What is an Evil Eye?" Onuma asked, amusedly.

Magic, apparently not knowing what the Evil Eye was, dodged the question.

"There are several remedies to choose from and my charges are low. You can have charmed rings from Arabia or oil from the Holy Ganges."

Onuma had heard this type of talk before and could estimate its worth. So he broke away from Magic's grip and started the car. As he drove away the occult doctor's voice pursued him. "Do not scorn *ogwu*. Political leaders, teachers and students cannot do without *ogwu*. Beware of the Evil Eye. . . ." He followed the car on foot until Onuma accelerated and left him standing far behind.

Onuma was looking forward to the next house he was going to visit, which had for him very pleasant associations. It belonged to Ire, a very old lady who in her time had been famous for her volubility. Her name had passed into proverb so that anyone who was a little too free with his tongue was labelled "Ire". Her own tongue had a sharp cutting edge but it was possible to take pleasure in being cut, for Ire had very little malice in her. She had a soft spot for the young and even though she chided them unmercifully she would always end

42

up by letting them take whatever oranges or pears they craved from her garden.

To Onuma's consternation and grief he found the famous tongue still. Ire was alive but in a sad state. of decline. Her daughter-in-law, a fairly aged person too, was with her and when Onuma was announced Ire didn't seem to remember him. She peered at him. "Whose son is he?"

"He is the son of ozo Udemezue Okudo. Surely, Mother, you know him. He loved oranges so much."

Ire seemed to be nerving herself up for one of her famous witticisms and Onuma was delighted to see once more a flash of the old fire.

"What does he wear a beard for?"

"It is the new fashion with the young," laughed the daughter-in-law. Ire lost interest again. The other woman whispered to Onuma, "The others are in the front house."

The others were her children and husband who lived in a new iron house in the forecourt of the compound. There didn't seem to be anybody in there when Onuma entered the living room. He clapped his hand and an impatient girl's voice asked, "Who is it?"

Onuma wouldn't announce himself but clapped again. "Come in here. Don't stand around clapping," the voice called.

Onuma opened the door of the room from which the voice came and was in a girl's bedroom. The girl was lying very still on a small iron bed. As he came in she looked up slightly and said, "Oh, it is you. Sit down."

Her name was Rita. Onuma remembered her as a gawky thin schoolgirl, but now she had filled out nicely and with a kind of shine which he knew from ex-perience indicated a passionate body. Onuma was too

43

much of a gallant to be put off by her cold reception of him after so many years. It was probably a technique she had fashioned for dealing with men. Or she may have been bored after a whole day without company. So Onuma smiled at her provocatively and refused to take her mood seriously. Gradually she began to take an interest in him.

"When did you come back?" she asked.

"A few days ago," he said.

"Oh," she said, and lapsed into a yawn. She said she was now a teacher in one of the villages and was home on holidays. Her younger sister who was at home was still in training also to be a teacher. He told her about Lagos. She took him up on a number of points and put him to rights. This combativeness was more in her style as he remembered. When young she had been of an independent fiery nature, a trait probably derived from her grandmother.

The evening was slowly yielding to night and Onuma suggested they go for a drive.

"Okay," she said, "but I will dress first."

"Do you want me to leave the room?"

"Do you want to?" She smiled patronizingly.

"No. You think I haven't seen a naked woman's body before."

"You are rotten," she said idly, "rotten to the core."

With not the slightest trace of self-consciousness she slipped off the rumpled dress she had been slumming around the house in and stood in her bra and panties. Onuma hastily took up a magazine nearby and began to read. "Say when," he said. A little moment later she said; "When." They walked to the car. "Oh, it is a Jag!" she said, trembling.

Onuma was taken aback by the remark. He had thought everybody knew. Surely the whole town had made a pilgrimage to the Udemezue compound to see the legendary car? People from towns many miles away had also come. It wasn't like her not to know.

She answered his unasked question. She had been away and had only just come back, she said. There was no elaboration and it crossed Onuma's mind with a tingle of jealousy that she must have been sleeping with another man. But he didn't mind now that she was all his. She was now signalling her subjugation and surrender in all sorts of ways. Whenever he looked at her she gave a small trembling smile which said: you can do anything you like with me. I trust you.

The Jaguar and the luxury and the power behind the luxury had overwhelmed her and drained her of any will. She couldn't resist even if she wanted to. And she didn't want to. She was content and fulfilled and at peace with the world. Onuma had seen this kind of response to his car before but he never ceased to marvel at the phenomenon; the power of a car on a girl. But why analyse and dissect the experience instead of simply enjoying it, he thought.

Onuma was heading for an isolated limb of the main road which led to the remote village of Obunagu.

"Where are you taking me to?" she asked.

"You are quite safe."

"I know I am safe," she said decidedly.

At a point in the road there was a clearing fringed on all sides by mango trees. He nosed the car into it and parked.

Darkness had taken over the day with dramatic suddenness and even Onuma was a little chilled by the vast emptiness of the surrounding countryside. Then suddenly there was a long drawn-out wail that appeared to come from the top of the car. The girl whimpered and clung to him. "What is it?" she asked nervously.

Onuma listened and said, "It's only a drum from up the hill."

"Oh," she said, a little relieved. "Let's go back."

"You will be okay."

"Please, Onuma. Let's go back."

He folded her in his arms, then took her upper lip between his teeth and savoured it. She clung closely to him and with smooth expertise wrapped her tongue around his.

"What do you want to do with me?" she asked.

"Guess."

"You want to fuck me?"

"I do."

"I know. You will mess me up and run away leaving me high and dry. I know."

Onuma was a little taken aback by the passion of her voice. But he didn't let it stop him. He led the way to the back of the car, she followed meekly and when they were there she carelessly kicked her shoes away and silently with ritual grace slipped out of her dress and curled up on the back seat. Onuma could see her eyes through the dark, gazing at him with mournful curiosity. When he went into her she shivered at the impact of his body, moved convulsively for a few moments, then went limp.

"What a to do," he thought afterwards as he drove back home. What a pointless exercise. He glanced at Rita resentfully. She had dozed off, her moist soft lips parted lazily.

The too, too, soft, easy slut, he thought. But his contempt did not last long. For as he looked at the perfect curves and the sensual glow of skin he began to yield to her feminine influence. His body once again yearned towards her. He leaned sideways, licked her parted lips and once again concentrated on the driving.

Onuma crowned the celebration by attending a dance held at Isu, the District Headquarters a few miles away. Dances with local bands supplying music were among the new ideas filtering in from the cities. They came in the wake of filling stations and pipe-borne water. With all these aids the small town of Isu advanced from a quiet backwater to a flourishing town. It had taken the first step to prosperity two decades or so ago with the building of three emblems of civilization, a government officer's bungalow with an adjoining football field for parades and bazaars, a post office, a police post with a prison. Then followed two grammar schools, one for boys and the other for girls, and finally an agricultural experimental station. Very soon small whitewashed iron houses clustered round these institutions. And the officers who occupied them and administered the district formed the local aristocracy. They earned more money than anyone else and new forms of entertainment had to be created to help them spend it. So a number of drinking bars sprang up, and one or two brothels. The Isu market, too, increased in sophistication. The young men from the surrounding villages who had become too well educated to follow the plough, having passed the elementary standard six, found a living as bicycle repairers, barbers, butchers and textile merchants. At about this time, too, there was talk of electricity, the ultimate status symbol for a town that had arrived.

The dance to which Onuma was going was organized by the enterprising owner of The Royal Dandy Hotel, which had a resident band.

According to the printed notices which had been scattered along the road from lorries, the dance was to start at eight o'clock in the evening, but Onuma made allowances for the vagaries of village timing and set out at ten. Just as he was getting out of Aniocha and was heading for Isu his attention was caught by repeated and prolonged brays. He stopped. Two young men, breathless, ran up to him. Onuma recognized Chuks, the taxi-driver.

"You are going to the dance?" Chuks asked.

"Yes," said Onuma. "Where is your taxi?"

"Gone for servicing. Broke down. We are coming with you." Chuks was breathing hard. His companion was a thin hairy youth dressed in a sort of leather jacket who had a broad smile permanently sketched on his face.

"Get in," Onuma ordered.

Chuks skipped into the front seat and his companion went into the back.

"We have been waiting for a bus since evening," continued Chuks, breathing hard. "At last we decided to walk."

"Walk five miles?" asked Onuma incredulously.

"Don't talk big," said the "revolutionary". "When you hadn't a car, you walked longer distances."

His companion guffawed. He seemed to guffaw at everything.

"I see you haven't brought any girl," commented Onuma as he raced through the night.

"No need to," breathed Chuks. "The band bring their own girls and you can take your pick. Well behaved girls from the city. Fine, fine girls."

"Haw haw," from the back.

The whole of Isu seemed to be attending the dance. They could not all be accommodated in the town hall where it was being held and which was fenced in with bamboo and palm leaves. The uninitiated stood outside gawking at their betters and making faces. The fence and the hall were illumined by coloured bulbs lighted by a mobile electric plant.

When Onuma and his friends arrived on the scene, the small entrance where the entrance fee was paid was packed with hordes of people fighting their way in. The local worthies, a magistrate, one or two lawyers and some well-to-do merchants stood aside from the crowd, gossiping in suave, distinguished circles. Onuma's first instinct was to imitate the quality and stay out until the crowd had thinned down. But Chuks and his friend had already fallen into the spirit of the struggle. Onuma fell in with them, elbowing, pushing and boxing his way through the vivid skirmish. Having hastily thrown his money in the face of some sweaty attendants he was catapulted unceremoniously, coat flying, into an ill-assorted mêlée. The open-air courtyard was swarming with people. There were young artisans on the prowl for excitement, women brought from the city who looked as if they would rather be somewhere else, and then the market mammies who were having their first taste of this kind of giddy living and were feeling quite hysterical about it.

Onuma, closely tailed by his partners, elbowed his way onto the dance floor. It was a white-walled space and now accommodated an infinite variety of humanity. The band played at one end. They were all dressed like red Indians. The leader, who also combined the roles of vocalist and first trumpet, carried the semblance of reality so far as to have a tomahawk slung across his shoulder. He performed all kinds of antics with his instruments. While playing the trumpet he would bend over backwards with his head almost touching the floor and sway from side to side to the highly vocal delight of the shuffling crowd.

49

The first thing Chuks did as they came into the hall was to head for the bar which adjoined the band and buy himself a bottle of beer. Then he wandered about drinking from the bottle and occasionally pouring some beer into the glass of his comrade in the leather jacket. Onuma was at first interested in watching the dancers, picking out future partners. He stood in one corner like a spider waiting for prey. After a while he became a subject of unashamed curiosity to the women. He saw several of them drag their partners to near where he was standing in order to have a good look. He was a past master at this type of game. To the women he didn't care for he gave a slight bow and smiled tenderly. But with those who challenged him and whom he desired he adopted an attitude of haughty scepticism. He still hadn't made up his mind which woman to take when Leather Jacket bumped into him. Onuma gave him a pound to go and buy beer. Leather Jacket merely went, handed over the money to the bar and came away with a bottle of beer.

"Where is the change?" Onuma asked sharply.

"The change?" said Leather Jacket, his face working up to a laugh.

Onuma walked him back to the bar with Chuks bolting after them. The place was manned by several anxious waitresses under the supervision of a big fat woman, the keeper of one of the Isu brothels. In addition to beer and soft drinks they also sold fried whole chicken. She had just given out one and was wiping her hand on her top wrapper when the three young men approached. She smiled encouragingly and favoured them with a full view of her extensive bosom which was well exposed above a low cut blouse.

Onuma explained to her the position. "You have our change."

"Whom did you buy from? Veronica, did these gentlemen buy beer from you?"

Veronica surveyed them suspiciously. "Of course not." She shrugged her shoulders. "Sisy, did these gentlemen buy beer from you?"

"Ask Beauty."

"Ask Angelina."

"Talk to Mama."

And then all the girls, seeing how confused the situation had become, giggled with pleasure. Onuma strode off followed by Chuks, berating Leather Jacket. The dance sequence had come to an end and the dancers shuffled out of the suffocating hall. Onuma, followed by his friends, made haste to get in front and snatch three of the few empty seats in the forecourt. They were not to occupy these undisturbed for long. Two couples towered over them with murderous expressions.

"Excuse me," one of them said harshly.

"What's the matter with him?" said Chuks, sensing a fight and eager for one.

"We were sitting here before," said the other man. "Can't you see our glasses and our bottles?"

The girls, local school teachers probably, looked at the intruders with inexpressible disgust.

"Our bottles were here before yours," said one of the newcomers.

"Eh?" asked Chuks.

"Take a walk."

"Its you who are going to take a walk," shouted Chuks, rolling up his sleeves.

The first man began to roll up his sleeves too. But the other, gauging the stature of their enemies, thought it would be wiser to withdraw with as much dignity as they could manage.

"Come on, Simon," he said in a very genteel voice. "Leave these ruffians alone."

"Besides we really don't want to sit. We can stand," the girls hissed with supressed hatred.

The other man, for appearance sake, made as much stand as he could, glaring murderously at his opponents and rolling up his sleeves, but at last he was dragged off by his impatient female partner.

There was a great deal of sleeve rolling among the people whose seats had been taken as they were dancing, and one or two fights actually broke out. The bellicose atmosphere was powerfully sustained by the crowd outside who could not pay their entrance. As far as they were concerned, to exclude full-blooded Isu people from the hall built by community labour was a patent injustice, so one or two would scale the fence with a view to jumping in. But just as they were getting ready to jump a local government policeman would come and give them a whack with his truncheon and they would collapse back into the midst of their companions. But they didn't give up the struggle. Towards the end of the dance they were to succeed in breaking the fence, getting a momentary glimpse of high life before the bubble dissolved in their faces.

Meanwhile the local worthies had actually come into the forecourt. They had taken staid tables at the corners and appeared to be the only stable elements in a restless mob.

Onuma ordered more beer and this time had to go and collect it himself. Chuks drank in avid mouthfuls, was soon tipsy and begun recommending Leather Jacket for a job with the firm which Onuma worked for.

"What can he do?" Onuma asked.

"Everything. He's been trained as a bricklayer in Enugu and can wire electricity in buildings. Not so?"

He slapped Leather Jacket roughly. The latter guf-fawed.

"He had better come and see me before I go back to Lagos," said Onuma grandly.

At that moment, there were shouts of "D.D.D!" and a short stocky man emerged waving to the crowd. He was the most promising young politician of Isu town and was usually appointed master of ceremonies in these weekend dances.

"Ladies and gentlemen, a cha-cha," he roared in a voice which was out of proportion to his small frame. Onuma staggered to the least objectionable of the girls from the city.

"No, you buy me beer first," she said.

"Okay," said Onuma.

"You promise?"

"You can have it after the dance."

But she wanted it before. Onuma took her to his table and called for another glass. Chuks gawked at her with tipsy, avid eyes. "How is it, daughter?" he asked fondling her knees.

"I beg, take your hands off me," she smiled. She had noted the many drinks consumed or available and was convinced that her host was a man of substance. This came as a relief after hours of being badgered by village louts. Her bitter mouth relaxed and she was all open. She had also forgotten all about the drink. "Come on," she said, "let's go and dance."

Onuma took her to the floor, crushed her with his big arms and shuffled her all over the room. She proved a talkative girl, wanting to know who he was, what he did and where his wife was.

"She's gone to her home," Onuma said solemnly. "We had a quarrel. She saw my secretary in my car," – he thought this a rather subtle way of bringing out the fact that he had a car — "and took offence. So now she is gone."

She was all commiseration. "Saw your secretary in your car and went? That was all? Oh what a silly thing to do. But of course it is just like us women. We can't think. Nevertheless you must go to her people and settle. You should go and apologize." She had discovered a very interesting way of getting to know him. But after some drinks and a few dances, Onuma was sorry that he had used this gambit. The girl was pretty or he would not have spoken to her, but too fresh. Her persistence in discovering him became a bore. He was glad when Chuks after several skirmishes prevailed on her to switch her interest temporarily to him.

Onuma's attention had been attracted by a magnificently ripe beauty who had been making frantic gestures to him all through the last dance. She was probably overripe for most people's liking but she would suit him. He walked into the hall holding a glass of beer in his right hand. The woman was there again, dancing with a fat paunchy man who smiled warmly at her all the time. Onuma remembered that during the dancing when his and her paths crossed she had always given a bright "come-along" signal. Now as he came around again she was smiling, offering herself.

"Excuse me. Dance?" Onuma cut in.

The paunchy man looked at him with great curiosity and then without saying a word relinquished her to him.

She smothered him with her sunny smile. They said nothing till the end of the dance then he took her to the table.

"Where has my husband gone? We don't want him to see us," she said. She flopped gracelessly but sensually on the seat and began to rearrange her head-tie.

54

She seemed to be all fluent eager flesh and Onuma's desire, already activated by the drinks, misted his eyes.

"Oh, there's my husband," she laughed melodiously.

The paunchy man had got hold of another woman. This one was staggering and appeared drunk. He led her out with rough indifference.

"That's my junior, his second wife," Onuma's woman smiled brightly.

"Let's go and take the air," he said.

"Oh," she said. Then she got up and smiled innocently into his eyes.

Onuma was glad he had parked his car at a remote corner close to the woods. As a matter of fact the possibility of his making a catch had been one of the factors in his deciding to park there. She showed no surprise at all about his subsequent actions. All their movements seemed to have been rehearsed. But although she moaned and wriggled with pleasure during his caress, when it came to the crucial part she said no. He pressed on. "No, no," she cried nervously, feebly restraining him. But when finally she had been stripped, she clung desperately to him. "Yes!" she cried. "Oh, yes!"

At the end she sprang up with a warm laugh, negligently rearranged her dress and smiled at him in a way that suggested, "Well, it's been such a treat." He made a face and she impulsively kissed the place where the forehead had creased. He took her back to the dance floor and she slipped quietly away.

When he returned to the table he found only Chuks and the girl. Leather Jacket had slipped away somewhere. Chuks had passed out. He had his face on the table. But when Onuma nudged him, the driver started mumbling an incoherent song.

The girl looked pityingly up at Onuma. She was still obsessed with that wife of his who had unreasonably left him for a trivial reason. She was determined to make up to him. And Onuma found himself warming up, starting the motions of courtship all over again. When he gauged that she was ready, he took her to the car.

The last girl he made that night was a schoolgirl who at the time he picked her up looked as if she had been on a long trek and had lost her way.

The band had stopped to catch their breath and suddenly the atmosphere assumed that deathly stillness of a solitary city that was once so full of people. The young artisans were still on the prowl, a little subdued by weariness and certainty of failure. The local worthies had all gone to their early beds. And the market women were quietly sleeping off the few glasses of beer they had taken. Onuma judged it was time to go. He had to drag Chuks up and for a few paces, before the latter recovered his bearings and staggered after him.

"Where is your friend?" Onuma asked.

"My friend, yah!"

Leather Jacket was waiting for them at the entrance and welcomed them with a special bray of laughter. Somehow he had managed to remain sober. When they got to the car Chuks spent an interminable minute trying to get into the driver's seat.

"That's my place," Onuma warned.

"Your place? Oh yes, your place."

"You go to the other side."

"Yah." Chuks strode into the night.

"Come back! Where are you going to?"

"Home! Going home. Going to chop life at home."

"Haw haw!"

Onuma drove up to him, "You better come in here if you don't want to walk five miles."

Chuks staggered blindly through the door held open

for him. All at once, with nothing leading up to it, he began extolling Onuma.

"Son of Udemezue Okudo, your father bore you well. You are famous in the ten towns, and in Lagos. Onuma, son of Udemezue Okudo, greetings. Rascals and idiots don't appreciate you but we know what you are about."

This praise for some reason exhilarated Onuma. "Yes," he agreed, "people of the bush don't know me but one of these days they must. I will plaster the whole world with currency notes. My name will be blazed round the world in millions of gold. My father is the first ozo of the land and don't let them forget it!"

At this juncture they came across an "off-licence" beer shop. Onuma crashed the car to a stop, staggered to the shop and came back carrying three bottles of beer all half uncorked. With some difficulty he handed two to his friends. Leather Jacket carefully recorked his and placed it gently by the corner of the back seat. Chuks drank a few mouthfuls and slopped the rest on the floor of the car.

Onuma drove with his right hand and drank with his left. It seemed to him that the car even went easier this way, driven with one hand. In the early dawn, with the headlights playing on the flimsy mist, he achieved a singular clarity of vision. The road seemed very straight with no ends. He was just swigging another mouthful of his beer when there was a suspicious swerve away from the road. For a short moment which at that time appeared like all eternity his mind misted and went blank.

On the Isu to Aniocha road, about a mile from the latter town, there is a steep precipice which descends sheer down for hundreds of feet. It is easily the most dangerous spot on the whole stretch of road, situated on a concealed turn over which careless drivers were endlessly crashing tragically. An unknown Aniocha wag, impatient with such cruel ineptitude, had planted a signpost against the chasm with the inscription: N O R O A D. But this didn't stop further fatal accidents.

Onuma's car had joined the others who had defied the N O R O A D sign. As a matter of fact the beautiful Jaguar had butted it out of the way and then went rolling happily on towards the chasm. But by one of those inexplicable strokes of luck which attend crazy people it had become wedged between two giant stones at the edge of the drop. There it hung, its nose in mid-air, its engine singing, while its wheels protested furiously. Onuma had the presence of mind to kill the engine. Then he burst out of the door, threw away the half empty beer bottle and crazily surveyed the wreck.

No one had been killed or hurt. And it is just possible that even the car might have been saved if Onuma had had the sense to leave it alone and go for sober help. Instead, what he did was to try and pull the car out of the wedge which sustained it.

"Lend a hand," he appealed to the night.

Leather Jacket came out and stood unconcerned, smiling.

"Lend a hand," Onuma called again, banging on the bonnet of the car.

"Oh," said a voice from within the car. "Oh, its you!"

Chuks tumbled through his door, came out, leaned on the panel and became sick.

"Lend a hand," Onuma shouted and, hanging on the back bumper, tugged desperately.

"*Eshobay!*" Chuks cried tipsily.

Leather Jacket took the cue and joined him, shouting, "*Ee!*"

"*Eshobay!*"

"*Ee!*"

And through their combined efforts the car was pulled back from between the stones. Immediately after it gave a happy skip, and just missing carrying the men with it, rolled down the precipice. There was finally a loud crash which signalled the end of one of the most elegant products of human craftsmanship in modern times.

Onuma at first made to go after the car but the crash had sobered him. Instead he stood for a minute gazing down at the ruin. Then, coming to a decision, he began to stumble home, but remembering that he had companions he returned to find Chuks leaning on one of the big rocks exhausted with the sickness. With the help of Leather Jacket Onuma bundled him out back to the main road.

Somehow they managed to walk the distance which remained to Aniocha and two hours later were standing beside Udemezue's heavily brooding compound. With terrific deliberation Chuks began to stumble home.

"Look out. Don't fall into the culvert," called Onuma.

"I will fall into the culvert if I want," said Chuks doing just that.

Leather Jacket went to help him out and away.

"Behave yourself," Onuma warned again.

"Go to hell," said Chuks.

8

Oliaku was full of anxiety when she brought breakfast to Onuma the next morning. She hadn't seen him since the previous day and she was longing to have a talk with him before he left for Lagos. He was still asleep when she came. But her coming awoke him. He came out of the bedroom dishevelled, unsteady and barely articulate.

"Greetings, Mother," he said through tight lips.

"Are you well?"

"It is nothing."

"I have brought you breakfast."

He glanced at the food with distaste but said, "Thank you."

She looked curiously at him. He exuded a heavy, sickly smell of alcohol. She didn't mind because from her long experience of Udemezue she knew men must get drunk once in a while.

She so much desired to have some serious talk with him – when was he going to get married, for instance. But she saw he was not in a condition for meaningful talk. So with patient resignation she put the food on a chair and walked back to her hut.

Onuma had a big headache and was sick of everything: the red-brown dying town, the sick-looking old men and their endless talk. He had an intense desire to punch somebody in the nose. The rage aggravated his headache even further so that it seemed as if a gang of tiny workmen were hammering on the inside of his skull.

What a fool, he thought, to have drunk so much the previous night, to have lost control and mastery! The women had had something to do with it. Women, he thought had always been the cause of all his failures. Knowing how weak he was, they exploited his ungovernable lust, his romanticism, his egotism. They would be his ruin. Still, he thought, it would be rather a good thing to have Rita just then. Her cool moist body would soothe his fevered limbs. Mentally he explored the imaginary bodies of some of the prettiest women he had had. Finally, to hell with women. To hell with everything, he thought.

Gradually his thoughts worked round to the events of the previous night. He had lost his beautiful Jag, his darling, the slave, the only one to whom he would ever be entirely attached. Oh, well one can always pick up another one. Insurance would see to that. But suddenly a thought shot across his befuddled brain. He had no insurance; it had expired a month before. The insurance company had written him suggesting some extravagant figure for a new premium. It was at the time he was raising money with which to celebrate at home. He had thrown the insurance company's letter away and forgotten about reinsuring.

"Oh my darling . . ." he was saved from the shame of wallowing in his own misery by a harsh voice he had come to know rather well these past weeks. It was Chuks the taxi driver. "Saved!" Shouted the voice again.

"Who is breaking my head so early in the morning?" roared the patriarch from his *obi*.

"Saved!" reiterated the taxi-driver.

"Will you shut your mouth, son of the bush!" bawled Udemezue sitting up on his white goat's skin.

"Oh, I am sorry, Father," said Chucks as if he had only just become aware of the patriarch. "Really sorry I am, Father."

But as soon as Udemezue turned away with a grunt he burst into Onuma's small house with another shout of "Saved!"

"Who is saved?" asked Onuma grimacing with pain.

"The car!"

"What! shouted Onuma jumping up and stepping uncertainly onto the tiny verandah where he glared at Chuks with bloodshot eyes.

"The car did not crash!" Chuks bawled.

"You are crazy—"

"It is you who are crazy. I saw it this morning. It is still intact."

"Come along, then," said Onuma striding out, still wearing his suit of the previous night.

"Aren't you going to put on your shoes?" Chuks asked.

"Oh, the shoes—" Onuma ran back to the room, and unsteadily put on his shoes, and then staggered out, dragging Chuks with him.

The hope of riding in his beautiful car again had cleared his head a bit, the tiny workmen in his skull had put up their hammers and were taking a rest. All that remained of his hangover was an unpleasant feeling of being sweatily hot and cold at the same time. Absorbed in his thoughts he gave offence to children and women returning from the common stream who said "good morning, sir," to him and received no response. His mind was closed to everything else but the car. He was indissolubly wedded to that car, his destiny was tied to it. The happiest, and most beautiful moments of his life that he could remember were spent in that car. He recalled vividly a debate he and his friends once had in his Lagos flat over the question of what each of them considered the most beautiful thing he had ever seen. One said a jet plane at the moment of take off, another opted for a new ship at rest. One girl even claimed that for her the most beautiful thing was a man's face at the point when he was having a climax on top of her. Onuma's unforgettable moment was driving in his new car at night through the Lagos Marina and viewing the myriad of lights carried by ships at port.

Onuma and his companion were soon at the chasm and then, precariously, holding on to boulders, climbed down and reached the car which was indeed still intact. There had been three miracles in the fateful incident of the previous night. The first miracle saved the three men from what should have been instant death. The second preserved the car after the first crash and the third provided it, in spite of the foolhardiness of Onuma and his hangers on, with a cushion in a small stream bed lower down the ravine. The crash that Onuma heard the previous night and which convinced him that all was over with the car was no more than the splintering of the windscreen and the headlight frames. The rest of the car, though slightly buried in mud, appeared as indestructible as ever.

Onuma first danced around the car caressing its muddy rump and kissing the fenders, as much of them anyway as he could get at. Next he jumped on the ragged Chuks, gave him a bear hug and then shook his own loins in obscene rhythmic movements against Chuk's.

"Saved!" he shouted. "My darling precious is saved."

"But how are you going to get it out of here?" the down-to-earth Chuks asked.

"Oh, we will push it out," said Onuma gasping from his exertions. "I will bring all the able-bodied men from Aniocha here to haul the car out. Come, let's go."

But there were decisive obstacles to his plan. Able-bodied men in Aniocha would haul a car only for a price and Onuma was becoming low in funds. Then it also became clear to Onuma that it was not really a job for men. Something else much more mechanical was needed to lift the car back to the road.

"If we could have some kind of crane," Onuma mused aloud.

"Crane?"

Onuma had almost forgotten that somebody was with him. He explained what a crane was.

"There won't be any here," said Chuks.

Obviously, thought Onuma. The nearest place where they would expect to see one would be thirty miles away at Onitsha. All of which pointed to the need to scrounge for money. Onuma would have to return to Lagos, the only place where money can be made. He decided that he would leave the next day, and told his parents as soon as he got home. There was a stir in the compound when he returned, an air of expectancy on the faces of even the children.

Chuks, before he came to wake Onuma up had assiduously spread the story. It was therefore to a despairing mother and an alarmed father that Onuma explained the situation. He was a little annoyed with their tragic mien although he himself had been driven almost crazy when he thought the car was gone. So he laboured to play down the extent of the accident. He tried to convince them that it was only a matter of time before the car would be back on the road. Udemezue nodded with sage relief. But it was left to the mother to sum it up in her woman's stoical way.

"The great God is just. I was sure He would not take away from us this one thing that we have achieved, this one thing we can hold on to in our bad and uncertain world."

PART TWO

Unreal City

1

Onuma was glad to be back on the road again. It was quite a change after months of luxury in his car for him to find himself in a ten-year-old smoky Mini, squeezed in between other smelly, garrulous passengers. The ordeal lasted only two hours. Then he had to transfer to a Peugeot wagon for the rest of the two hundred mile run. The Peugeot's performance over this route had become legendary for the hell-bent speed with which the drivers operated and the casualty rate. One of the prime attractions of the journey was the sight of carcases of lorries and cars caught in the crooked death traps called bridges. At one spot a woman's body swollen to twice its life size lay by the wayside, its skin peeling off in the mid-day sun. Somebody quite unnecessarily pointed out the grisly details causing several people to stick their heads out to gape at the scene. For a few minutes after that everyone was hushed and chastened. Then the chatter resumed on other subjects than that which troubled everyone in that taxi. It was as if they wished by mere volubility of utterance to drown the memory of the nightmare they had just been through. There were often stray corpses on this death trail. Everybody did their best not to notice, to forget. After a week or so the bodies disappeared as mysteriously as they had appeared; and this fact in itself seemed to justify everyone's attitude of leaving well alone.

Except for a couple of hair-breadth escapes the journey was relatively uneventful and they crunched into Lagos in the early dusk of a Sunday. At this time of the day it was half-deserted, could let down its hair and enjoy a respite from the heavy crowds that sallied out to display their best clothes earlier in the day and the throngs that would haunt the pleasure spots later on. There were clusters of people still abroad, mostly daringly dressed teen-age girls whose energy and lust for activity enabled them to bridge the two actions.

Onuma stepped down from the bus with the kind of pleasant trepidation with which he always approached this town. There Lagos was, his town. The landmarks were as familiar to him as his brown cat's eyes seen in a mirror. The stink of Lagos, too, was pervasively familiar, a potent compound of decaying fish, stale urine and days-old shit. But the luxury cars, the Mercedes Benzes, Cadillacs, cruised along as if to belie the stench. And the girls lounging about wanting to be picked up were as slickly dressed and as sexy as ever. Onuma cast around for a face he knew. It had always happened in the past that wherever in Lagos there was a crowd of people in which girls predominated, one of them would turn out to have been to bed with him at some time. And, sure enough among the crowd he saw near a bus-stop there was a girl he had once had. Onuma remembered her vividly as a lost girl who, out of desperation, had given so much of her self to him. At the time he met her she had only just left school, come to Lagos from the country and begun "to go wrong". On the day he picked her up with his Jaguar she had been thrown out of her rented shack in the slum area of the city. That night in return for a roof over her head she had surrendered her hard fresh body unconditionally. After each of several bouts of lovemaking, she would blubber about how "I have become so bad. They warned me at home that Lagos is bad for me, but I wouldn't listen. Oh, my God!" But after a while she would turn to him and plead that she was "high" and that he could punish her again, please, if he wished. Which he did.

The memory of her in bed gave a keen edge to the second encounter with her and Onuma made vigorous signs to attract her attention. But she was curiously blind and deaf to his motions. He would have continued to gesticulate until she noticed, but just then a young man in a Citroen stopped by her, to the vocal disapproval of the crowd at the bus-stop.

"Big man for noting abi you no see? This place na bus stop!" one shouted.

"No Minam. E tink say na only 'im wey sabi drive Citroen!" grumbled another.

"Big man debtor, why you no commot?"

The Citroen owner seemed oblivious of these taunts. With an imperious gesture he beckoned to Onuma's girl. She walked up to him with a wiggly grace which Onuma supposed she must have learnt since leaving him, and then with practiced nonchalance opened the door of the Citroen and stepped in. The Citroen owner rushed off with ostentatious screeching of tyres.

"Ole! Thief!" shouted the bystanders. But the man got the girl, thought Onuma. Which is what mattered. The incident impressed on Onuma the strange magic of the car. It not only gave a man standing, it made everything possible, love, hope, joy, charity. The car was the man. Without a car he was crippled, and that girl had no time for cripples.

Before the incident Onuma had been debating in his

mind whether to join the harsh bus crowd or take a taxi. A taxi obviously was expected of a man of his stature, a man who only a few days before had floated on the crest of the wave of a Jaguar car's luxury; but his funds had run out, there was no way in which the money in his pocket could pay for a taxi to his house. But the incident of the Citroen decided him. He would take a taxi if it killed him.

All through the drive, he sat fascinated by the click of the meter. What if it overran the limit of his purse. He was just calculating how to pacify the taxi driver in case he had to underpay him when the taxi approached Ikeja, his destination, and Onuma saw he could pay the fare with a few pennies to spare. There was a short distance still to go over broken dirt road. Friends who were solicitous of their vehicles often baulked at going through this last bit when they visited, but Onuma had been taking the Jaguar over it for months. But for his being in so weak a bargaining position he would have made the taxi driver take him right to his doorstep. As it was he had to carry his luggage and stumble through the mud. One spot was particularly noisome. There was a permanent pool of muddy water caused by a burst pipe at the base of a house belonging to a retired senior civil servant. Several people who lived on the street, not least Onuma, had on several occasions remonstrated with this man. But the man, insulated within his self-importance, not only would do nothing but was affronted that lesser mortals, and in Onuma's case younger ones, dared to fault him. There was an unwritten code in Lagos according to which important people, or at least those who considered themselves important, were immune from criticism no matter what crime they committed.

The other landmark of the street, and the source of

the neighbourhood's stench, was a huge common trash dump. Though the dirt road was duly registered with the city authorities at great personal cost to the local worthy after whom it was named, it still did not enjoy the attention of city trash removers. So the people on the street simply threw their trash out of the window. It started with two men building a small dump on an open space near their houses. The spot soon attracted everybody and a large open trash dump grew and festered. Several of the neighbourhood children who had no toilet facilities in their houses also used the dump. Indeed as Onuma was passing by, a small naked girl squatted on the garbage performing her toilet. Onuma had often seen shit around the dump but had never encountered the culprits. Feeling a little sick he made a frantic gesture as one who would shoo away a pig. But the small girl in the throes of defecation merely stared at him with glassy sick eyes. Onuma angrily turned away, hating himself and the world that allowed such sights to becloud the day.

The house in which Onuma lived appeared an island of elegance in a sea of filth. It was a spruce two-story mansion of four apartments. Onuma had chosen it because of its elegance and its cheapness − a house of such quality in the developed area of the town would have rented at three times as much as Onuma paid for his flat. The landlord's motive in investing in the slum neighbourhood appeared to be the hope that development, however slow, would sooner or later catch up with the area.

To his amazement and no small irritation Onuma was welcomed home warmly, too warmly, by his next-door neighbour, a buxom widow. There had been an acre of thin ice between them ever since she had to send away her nubile teen-age daughter to boarding school, apparently to escape his influence. The widow's attempt at breaking the ice was linked to the fact that she had only recently fallen out with the gentleman who lived in the upstairs flat, an unsuccessful lawyer who had been pitifully striving to exact respect and recognition from sceptical neighbours. Relations between him and Onuma had not been helped by the Jaguar which reflected badly on the other man's ten year old Volkswagen beetle. The lawyer had occasionally employed chauffeurs to tip the balance, as it were, but found he couldn't pay them. His slaves came and went roundly cursing him and further undermining his security. The lawyer had previously been very chummy with the widow in an attempt to isolate Onuma, and his falling out with her subsequently was only a further sign of the man's frustration. All the same Onuma had deep reservations about any collusion with the widow. For one thing he still could not forgive the old cow for spiriting away her daughter, a freshly ripened peach which he had been on the point of plucking. So he played cool to her warmth but the widow was too deep in her strategem to notice. Before she left him she directed a loud blast of laughter at the lawyer. Her enemy stood at the front porch in his usual house clothes, a wrapper topped by a singlet, and had been contentedly cleaning his teeth with a bit of stick and spitting the bits downstairs. The widow's laughter made its point. The lawyer dodged back into his living-room before its echo had died and she had emerged to gauge its effect on him.

The racket she had created awakened Onuma's houseboy, majordomo, floor-mat, tool, critic and walking conscience. He emerged from his room with his all-purpose smile and fussed over the one bag which his master carried. Onuma shrugged him away and then for lack of something better to say asked: "You have been sleeping, Friday?"

"Yes, sir."

He seemed always to be sleeping and never took the trouble to deny it: too drowsy or too sure of himself, or just too uncaring. It was in the nature of their relationship that Onuma must exchange some local gossip with him. Anyway the boy seemed to expect it.

"Anybody asked for me?" Onuma asked, by way of beginning.

"Na, only madam."

Which madam could this be? Onuma wondered. The widow? The owner of the beer shop round the corner whose account was over-due?

"Na, Gloria," Friday hastened to add. "E come sleep here for yesterday."

Yes, Gloria, Onuma's current girl, had a key to the flat. She often needed to escape from the fetid room in the slums where she vegetated with her grandparents. Gloria was entrusted to the old people's care by her parents who lived up country and the old people took the charge very seriously. As Gloria told it they went wild whenever she slept out with Onuma or with anybody else. Having existed in stench and squalor for close on a century, and having even come to love it as a pig loves a specially noisome favourite burrow, they were incapable of understanding a young girl's compulsive itch to escape to the bright lights she saw everywhere, even if she had to barter her body to do so. Gloria would break into giggles when she described her battles with them. She always won because they needed her more than she needed them. They couldn't live without her. They couldn't stand each other's company for long. Boredom and loneliness had broken the human link that joined them and they needed Gloria both as a sustenance and as a buffer between their mutual antagonisms.

Onuma hoped Gloria would be back that night, and was glad. She would have to help him out of his housekeeping straits that day and what is more would do it with consummate tact. Gloria was one of the rare girls in Lagos who guessed when the burdens of city life were weighing a man down and helped him without eroding his self-esteem. Most girls felt bewildered and hurt, humiliated, when any of the men they slept with failed to live up to the role of bill-payer and provider.

"Did Gloria say she would come again tonight?" Onuma asked.

"She no say anything." Friday shrugged.

Gloria was not one of Friday's favourite people. None of Onuma's girls seemed to hit it off with Friday. Friday still retained his peasant notions of propriety and a suspicion of city women whom he regarded as gold-diggers out to rob his master.

Onuma dismissed him with an impatient gesture but the boy had not nearly done. He stood shifting from one leg to another and at last blurted out "Nothing de for house." This was said with an air of long-suffering martyrdom. Friday never passed up any chance to improve his fortunes, thought Onuma, who had left him money enough to last for the period he would be away. But from Friday's perspective Onuma was an almost unlimited source of wealth, and one which owed him a lot and doled it out in niggardly bits. There was an onus on Friday's ingenuity to devise methods of exacting his due. So in spite of Onuma's impatient "Take yourself away from here", Friday stood his ground in an attitude of self-righteous oppression until his master, himself oppressed by the boy's presence, stormed into his bedroom slamming the door.

The bedroom, furnished lavishly, always served him as a refuge where he and his girls could indulge in mutual therapy against the frenetic contradictions of the city. After a short while the room began to work its soothing effect. Surrounded by well-loved and familiar things Onuma recovered a sense of his proper self, a certainty about his place in the shifting scenes of life. Only one element was required to complete his recovery, a woman. Generally at this time of night he made love. All of the tensions of the city would have been building up to it. Love became a release. Women would generally come to him. If they didn't, he drove about: to YWCA centres where bored lodgers hankered for action, to one-room tenements in the slums which miraculously spewed out some of the loveliest butterflies in town. How could good come out of such foulness? He had frequently asked himself this question without finding an answer. How did some of these girls, bred in the putrid miasma of the gutter, emerge clean, lissome, and fresh, all the curves on them in the right places? If he lived in any one of the slum areas of the city for a week he would go mad. And yet these girls endured it for years without any visible taint, or a diminishing in appetite, or failure of their uncanny instincts for the gestures that gave spice and promise to life. As Onuma dwelt more and more on thoughts of these, and of Gloria especially, he began to go erect and rigid which made the night a torture. But finally he slept and had Gloria only in his dreams, in one of which he was trying futilely to push into her as both of them flew winglessly through the air.

2

It was going to be one of those mad, mad Mondays in
Lagos, when motor traffic was snarled up all over the
town in hot, murky despairing stretches. The people
who owned cars all observed the ritual of the beginning
of the week with religious fervour. On Monday, after
the week-end interruption, they resumed the grim
scramble for crusts that fell off the tables of the great
of the earth. They needed cars for the struggle not
merely as a practical lever but as a psychological crutch.
So they killed themselves to buy these cars. But the
cars arrived before there were roads to ride them on. So
the first battle was fought over control of bits of the
road in Lagos.

Onuma entered the fray at its dustiest and most
frenetic point, being forced down to the ranks by a
state of being with which he wasn't entirely unfamiliar
– penury. Onuma was aware and marvelled at a re-
current pattern in his life, a cyclical movement of order
and chaos often reflected in a regular sequence of
periods of personal affluence followed by utter penury.
There seemed no way of breaking the vicious circle.
Wise men would urge him to save for the rainy day,
but would they ever show him how to reconcile his
highly inflamed expectations with the pinched life which
the country had to offer him? Having lost his lovely
car he should have had the means to travel in elegant
fashion by taxi. But he hadn't. He couldn't even afford
any of the new smart buses which had recently stretched
their itinerary to include places in the city as remote as
Ikeja. Instead he was forced to wait on a ghostly thirty-
year-old truck which whizzed and puffed a noisome
ball of smoke into the air. When he arrived the bus was
almost full, so Onuma had to fight to get in. He did

74

find himself what appeared to be the very last of the seats whose springs showed and bit into the travellers' bottoms.

All the seats had now been taken but the driver of the bus was in no hurry to move, which prompted someone to mutter: "Which kin people be this? Driver abi you no de go?"

The driver, ensconced in a little box in front, peeped back and announced with a tolerant smile: "Na conductor you go ask dat one."

The conductor, a dour young man in ragged *agbada*, was standing at the steps of one of the back doors wolfing down a piece of bread. He had learnt through experience to ignore passengers who urged him to move before he had filled up every available cranny in the bus. The heat of the early morning flowed into the bus and seemed to claim all the passengers in a clammy inexorable hug. For a while the usual bus travellers' chatter, the usual vocal review of the latest smut story in town, was hushed.

Onuma's neighbour was a bewigged beauty who squirmed from the heat.

"Conductor you no go die well!" she shrieked, as sweat coursed down her lovely face in ochre-coloured rivulets.

"Wetin?" growled the conductor, dropping the rest of the bread he had been eating.

The girl was unimpressed.

"Abi you no see the bus don full?" she hurled back at him.

He took it up.

"The bus don full? So? I no go eat my bread finish?"

This was too much for the passengers. They fell on him.

"Na bread you come eat here?" – "You no cu-cu

75

eat for your house?" – "Who givam the job sef?" – "Why they no sackam one time?" – "Son of shit!"

The conductor, for the moment overwhelmed, sulked but would not give the order to go.

He let them sweat a bit longer, then struck languidly at the rattling side of the bus and shouted "Go on!" But by then it was too late: the great Lagos traffic jam had caught up with the travellers. The other passengers accepted the situation with hushed fatalism, but Onuma was too oppressed by the heat and the smell of the sweaty crowd and a nagging sense of failure to stay in the bus any longer. Having come to a quick, characteristically impulsive, decision he got out of the bus and walked. The long hopeless queue stretched nose to bumper for what appeared miles. Behind the wheels Onuma recognized the Lagos car-owning types: the new entrants to the club, identified by their age and by their harassed faces, a manner disoriented by debts and exacting mistresses; and the businessmen with "beer-beer" paunches, so-called because they were supposed to be a mark of the kind of affluence which could afford large potations of beer. Onuma disliked the latter's smug mediocrity and derived a savage joy from thinking about the contemptuous terms which some of the Lagos gold-diggers he had had free applied to such men after milking them.

It was still not possible to locate the cause of the jam, though in these Monday morning mix-ups there was often no obvious bottleneck, just confusion, loss of control and the impossibility of accommodating the competing interests of too many hungry people.

A niggling noise had been assailing Onuma's ears. Onuma knew the source of the noise. He had caught a brief glimpse of him through the window of a Mercedes and had quickly averted his face and elaborately concentrated his attention on a brick structure that abutted on the street. But the noise – low whistling and jeering words – continued. Onuma could hear his name being called but he remained absorbed in the brick structure and would not respond. The source of the noise Onuma knew to be a young snob of his acquaintance. Onuma wasn't going to take a ride in the fellow's car, only to be used to measure how far up the Lagos social ladder the idiot had come. The traffic chaos intensified. Some of the drivers, in a desperate effort to force their way through the jam, had run athwart the lines or jumped into the side track used by pedestrians, creating more chaos. The deadly prospect loomed of Onuma having to walk the full fifteen miles to Lagos. He was mentally preparing himself for the long, hot dusty ordeal when he heard again the whistles and the jeering call.

Well, maybe it would not be such a bad idea after all, thought Onuma as he approached the Mercedes which had managed somehow to break out of the snarl. His surrender was glossed over by insincere gestures of mutual courtesy, by gestures of false good fellowship.

"How is the car doing?" asked the owner of the Mercedes, trying desperately to mask his deep curiosity by deadly concentration on his driving. "What is a man who used to own a Jaguar doing walking the streets of Lagos?" he thought.

"Oh, the car is gone for servicing," said Onuma with glib ease. Let the fellow work out the puzzle for himself.

"You weren't at the last Island Club dance," continued Mercedes, giving Onuma a sharply speculative look as if measuring the extent of his fall from the grace represented by a Jaguar.

"Dinner with my chairman," parried Onuma.

"The party was extra special," boasted Mercedes. "So many high-ups were there that day, Alhaji Siaka, chairman of the Board of Ikeja Cements. And also the Prince, Senior Assistant Secretary. Oga man! A high-up tells me the Prince will soon be a Permanent Secretary. The boy is good bo! There were many many other high ups there, I cannot remember all. And girls were *borku*. Estella asked about you."

"Which Estella?" asked Onuma in a tone whose flippancy he hoped would discourage the joker, for he was not in the mood to share Estella or Estella's reputation with him. But Mercedes was in too full steam to be checked.

"How do you mean, which Estella? Estella! Is there another Estella?" He was not so much puzzled as suspicious. Apparently Onuma's failure to react to the name Estella deepened the mystery of his going without a car. He cast another speculative look at Onuma's dusty shoes as if there lay the clue.

Onuma saw he must play out this game of mutual boasting which characterized the conversation of young men in Lagos.

"Oh, Estella," he said in a bored, worldly-wise voice. "What is her problem?"

"I think I. K. has sacked her. She just goes from one man to another and they fuck her out. But she survives. Great survival instinct, that girl has. You know I used to go with her sister? Nothing serious though, just fucker friendship."

The words seemed wrenched out of Mercedes and chucked out of the window into the clammy dawn, for at that moment he had to swerve desperately to avoid an old garbage truck which had lumbered out from nowhere and blocked the way, blowing a thick cloud of noisome fumes straight in their faces.

"You bungling rats!" exploded Onuma. "You cockroaches!"

"You carriers of shit!" chimed in Mercedes, killing his engine and screeching to a halt. Simultaneously the two young men burst out of the car and while Onuma stood glaring at the garbage truck with hatred, Mercedes excoriated them in language any Iddo motor-part tout would have been proud of.

"You shit-encrusted untouchables, you who shame the road, do you think to have a brake in a car is a luxury? You sons of the garbage heap!"

Only a huge billow of smoke from the broken exhaust answered, driving the two men back, choking.

The driver of the truck kept it on the rev for a few more minutes before he blew a loud, impudent finale. Meanwhile his assistant, who had been perched on the tailboard, scrambled down, expertly removed one of the rear tyres, laid it on the ground as a pillow, and went to sleep.

God, in his infinite mercy, would take care of everything.

The drama went through its hysterical course. Hordes of impatient drivers behind them hooted furiously, raising a swirl of dust and noise that accentuated the manic mood of the crowd. Policemen appeared, berated the driver of the old truck, kicked awake his assistant, made useless notes, attempted despairingly to control the chaos and then, unable to do so, sneaked away trailed by a flak of complaints and abuse from frustrated commuters.

The road was all but unusable. The delinquent truck had blocked one side of it. But both oncoming and ongoing traffic could take turns at using the one free lane and this they did with often disastrous consequences. During one particularly ugly tie-up Onuma decided that he would assume the role of traffic warden and honest, but not too honest, broker. There was no problem in gaining the cooperation of the motorists, for they had reached such a level of frustration that they were ready to yield leadership to anyone who offered any kind of solution, no matter what. Onuma succeeded in facing down a few violent crazies and tranquillizing other hysterical ones with soft words. In a moment the traffic could trickle through the small gap he had created and Mercedes, who proved a pastmaster in the art of muscling in and taking hair-breadth risks, was able to get through. Onuma relinquished his self-imposed task and joined his friend and they spent the rest of the drive in a viciously nihilistic appraisal of the city of Lagos.

What with the trials of the day and nagging anxiety Onuma was not at his best when he sought out the manager of his bank and asked for an over-draft. The manager turned him down flat without saying why. He had read in Onuma's face signs of need and desperation. His instincts were dead against needy and desperate people. They were bad news. He avoided them as he would avoid the plague.

The bank was owned by a European company which was generally believed to milk Nigeria. The manager who authorized over-drafts was a Nigerian. His refusal to do a favour to a fellow Nigerian signified to Onuma collusion with the enemy to victimize the black race. The man was a stooge. Onuma's hackles rose not only against being denied relief but also against potential ideological treachery.

"I will close my account with you!" he shouted.

The manager was tolerant. "Oh, that would be a pity," he answered. "But what can we do? You see, Mr Okudo. . . ."

"My name is not Mr Okudo."

"I'm sorry. . . ." The manager looked at his ledger to make sure, but before he looked up again, Onuma strode angrily out.

In a moment he stood before a fat cashier and furiously demanded to have his account closed. The fat cashier reciprocated with disdain and hostility.

"And what is your name?" she asked with a bitter curl of the lips.

Onuma none too graciously announced his name and account number, and waited. After what seemed an age a sad uniformed messenger brought a slip. The fat cashier glared at it and then, looking up at Onuma with elaborate calm, announced:

"Your account is red. To close it you have to pay the bank three pounds and five shillings for checking fee. Next person, please."

There was little chance of leaving the place with dignity but Onuma did try. Putting on the manner of one injured beyond endurance he swung round haughtily and swept out of the bank. He built up enough momentum out of his rage to carry him to his place of work, the Anglo-Nigerian Shipping Company, while he was in an unconscious daze.

Mr Karolides welcomed him with bland courtesy. "You had a good holiday?"

"Oh well. . . ." Onuma failed to complete the sentence and Karolides did not press him. That damned tact of his! Onuma was on the point of narrating his problems but checked himself, defeated by the other man's impersonal attitude. Mr Karolides did not encourage sharing of confidences and personal woes. His relationship with his staff, especially the Nigerians, was strictly on a keep-your-distance official level. They didn't know where he lived, if he had a family or not, what his love life was like. The same bland mystery shrouded his shipping business. It was the job of Onuma to sell the business to the Nigerian public, but he never saw any ships. There were some he heard of, which were hired from established lines and operated what looked very much like smuggling. But you couldn't imagine Mr Karolides engaging in clandestine activities. He appeared much too solid. His manner, more than that of anyone Onuma had ever known, suggested the strict, narrow path. Onuma hated and admired him for the completeness and effectiveness of the façade of innocence he presented to the world.

When Mr Karolides smiled blandly and waved him away, Onuma went almost automatically to the company's accountant, Mr Koko. Mr Koko was not reticent about his or the company's private affairs. He was prolix, expansive and bawdy. He seemed especially buoyed up by having a captive audience to share vicariously in his business and sexual successes. His latest conquest, he now told Onuma, was a young school-girl barely past her teens. He had won her affection by promising her a job. And knowing there wasn't going to be any job – because of course only the *oga*, meaning Mr Karolides, could give jobs – Koko said he had spent a great deal of money to dazzle her. He had flown her from the north and set her up in a lavish hotel in Lagos and then painted a rosy picture of her prospects in the job! In gratitude she had been giving him the most dazzling sexual performance he had ever had.

"Why," he boasted, "last night she nearly killed me. Where do these girls learn how to fuck?" However, the girl had a big surprise coming to her, Koko said.

"You see she claimed she can type. They all do. I know she cannot. I have tried her. I want to see her face when I bring her to the office tomorrow, give her a test and then, when she fails, kick her out. Before that, of course, I shall swim again in her big hairy arse. Have you ever had the experience of sacking a girl just after fucking her?"

"As a matter of fact, no."

Koko was anxious to hear all about Onuma's own experiences but Onuma wouldn't oblige him. He was under the influence of another kind of fixation that morning.

Koko snatched the opportunity for boasting which Onuma had passed up, and started displaying his business affairs, the frustrations of building two houses at the same time and paying the school fees of three of his nephews in grammar school.

"And, you know, my account in the bank is never in the red."

"Really?" said Onuma genuinely interested this time.

"Oga has been good to me. He gives me a loan each time I ask for it."

This was a cue for Onuma to advance his own needs. He inquired about the possibility of a loan.

Koko clammed up at once. His expansive manner gave way to a distracted busyness; the black moist eyes of a practiced womaniser clouded, he bent his handsome bushy brows in a painful attempt at concentration on a big ledger and in a changed voice reminded Onuma of a long-standing credit.

"You took five hundred pounds for 'entertainment' and I haven't received your expense record. Do you have it now?" He glanced at Onuma with bitter reproach. He had always resented the fact that someone else in the company enjoyed the benefits of an expense account and not he.

The ringing of the telephone at that moment had the effect of pacifying him a little. His manner over the phone was eager and unctuous and his replies with many sirs indicated he was talking to Mr Karolides. At the end he hung up and his eyes shone with devotion. In a voice which still retained a little quaver he announced: "That was *Oga*." Then in a much sharper voice he asked, "Do you know where we can buy foreign exchange?"

Onuma's heart missed a beat. He had at once a premonition of a movement in his life that was going to be decisive and terrible. The feeling passed in a moment. And then he heard Koko asking: "Can you take one of our boys to purchase?"

Onuma hesitated, and Koko had recourse to the magic password: "*Oga* asked me to talk to you."

"There is no way," said Onuma. "I have to go alone."

Koko flashed dark suspicion at Onuma, then brooded a little. Finally he mumbled: "Anyway you are still on holiday and we shouldn't impose on your private time."

Onuma ignored this puerile doodling. His mind was somewhere else, watching his car, his *alter ego*, the symbol of his personal identity come alive again. He wondered what Mr Karolides needed the foreign exchange for at this time. Buying foreign exchange from the black market to take back to Britain was a common tax dodge, it concealed surplus earnings which European companies operating in Nigeria were not so keen on declaring to the Internal Revenue Service.

Buying foreign exchange was so essentially one of Onuma's duties that he wondered why Koko hesitated about entrusting it to him.

"How much is involved?" Onuma asked in what he hoped was a level voice.

"Two or three hundred," said Koko reluctantly, watching Onuma carefully.

"And when?" asked Onuma keeping the disappointment from his voice; he had hoped it would be much more.

"Today or tomorrow, I expect," answered Koko in the same doubtful voice. He presented an appearance of having lost interest in the project and of wishing the interview to end. Actually this was his usual reaction to any company project from which some other person could get a cut.

Onuma, alarmed at seeing his chance slipping away, played his trump card.

"I shall be away from home tomorrow."

"Oh there is no hurry," said Koko airily. "It can wait till you return."

"But I don't know when I will be back. Wait, let me go and talk to Mr Karolides about this."

This tactic worked. Koko could not disguise his alarm. The matter was being taken out of his hands. His capacity to receive *Oga's* message and pass it on was in question. He must retrieve the initiative.

"I will make out a cheque," he announced as if coming to a sudden dramatic decision.

"Come here!" he barked in the direction of one of the clerks in the adjoining office. The boy rushed to him.

"Make out a voucher for three hundred pounds to Mr Okudo. . . ." As if as an afterthought and to dampen the pleasure which had begun to light up Onuma's face he added: "We will have to give it to you as a loan from a special account and receipt it this evening when you bring in the foreign exchange."

Onuma could not but acquiesce. He waited with an inner glow and expectation which he hoped was not too apparent while the cheque was prepared and while Koko, now a bitter and harassed man, went to Mr Karolides' office to have it countersigned. Koko's humour was still not improved when he returned. Onuma had

85

mistaken a gesture of his as a willing offer of the cheque and was stretching his hand to take it but Koko quickly withdrew his hand. "You haven't signed yet," he said icily.

Onuma signed, received the cheque, flashed a taunting smile at the accountant and bolted before he had time to change his mind.

"Get dollars if you can but otherwise sterling will do," Koko bawled after him. Onuma barely heard him, for he was already in dreamland, floating on the crest of the wave of a happy re-union with his beloved.

First he cashed the cheque at the bank, then he had to rehabilitate himself from the traumas of the day as well as to celebrate.

He repaired to the lounge of the Hotel Glasgow and ordered beer. It was a busy time of day and there were lots of well-dressed young men doing deals, people of strictly small stakes. They all carried black brief-cases as a kind of badge of honour. A few pretty young prostitutes hung around taking small pickings here and there. The Hotel Glasgow had started out many years before as an exclusive resort for white men and well-heeled black business partners. Now in response to the egalitarian notions of the times it had thrown open its doors and become a combination of stock market and brothel. Deals were made here, pimps and prostitutes picked out clients, under-the-counter operations were carried out.

Onuma had hardly settled to his beer when he was approached by a thin young man whose prospects for success were hampered by an atrociously cut suit. Onuma nevertheless smiled at him encouragingly. He had seen him many times before in just such surroundings and although Onuma had never spoken to him the young man always regarded him very familiarly. Onuma wondered whether all he wanted was free beer and was determined not to give it to him. But the newcomer settled in easily, deposited his brief-case carefully and then quite calmly and boldly asked if Onuma wanted to buy foreign exchange.

"Dollars or sterling?" Onuma asked.

"Dollars, but if you want sterling it can be arranged."

"No, thanks."

The young man smiled ingratiatingly in a no-offence-meant way and, grabbing his brief-case, went to solicit elsewhere.

When Onuma reached home later in the evening he found Gloria already in his bed. She looked ridiculously small tucked in under a gold-coloured wrapper. Her honey-coloured skin combined with the gold of the cloth to set up a glow that illumined the half-dark of the bedroom.

Onuma's body was already rigid by the time he was down to his drawers. She had been pretending to be asleep but when he began hastily to strip away the wrapper she showed she hadn't been asleep by commenting: "You don't talk to me about home or anything, but the first thing you want to do is fuck."

Oh how charmingly characteristic of Gloria, he thought as he continued his tender delicate manœuvres. It would be impolitic to talk now. For Onuma understood Gloria. Essentially she had two personalities. One was bruised by the slums and the hard struggle to survive in Lagos – the wounds were healed but left numerous scars which still hurt when rubbed the wrong way and it was not always easy to discern the right way. The other personality, which emerged during and after lovemaking, had no neuroses and seemed entirely compounded of sweetness and light. The memories which constituted his love for her had to do with his sense of wonder at the emergence of this other sensibility. So he set to work and within minutes had roused her to a peak of incoherent ecstacy. At the end they could talk and gossip and make plans in the magic afterflow of shared orgasm.

3

When Onuma arrived at the Iddo motor park the next morning he had to undergo the serious manhandling which appeared mandatory for all prospective travellers.

A number of motor park touts rushed at him. One relieved him of his luggage, others of his coat, and yet a third hustled him to a Peugeot wagon. By using his fists and tongue to the best effect he was able to recover some balance and find a place in a Peugeot of more or less his own choice. But the touts who had rustled him were very good-natured about it all. For them passenger-rustling was an egalitarian ritual and giving and taking knocks was an inescapable part of it. As one of them remarked to Onuma, amiably: "If you no wan make we touch you make you go buy your own car."

Onuma's heart leapt to think that within a matter of some hours he would indeed have his own car and be free from the contamination of the motor parks. But what would happen if the Jaguar was not salvaged? Onuma pushed the thought quickly away, he could not bear to think of such an overwhelming eventuality. His hand stretched out protectively on the cardboard box containing some expensive motor parts he had bought in expectation of the repairs. He knew that the parts would not be obtainable anywhere else in the country except Lagos.

The road going back was not as empty and as menacing as before, having already taken its usual toll of blood from unwary travellers. The bloated corpse had been carted away by anonymous samaritans. Within a few hours the Peugeot squeezed its way into the hoardes of clamorous dusty people at the famous Onitsha market.

Onuma extricated himself from the heady mass of unwashed flesh and taking a sixpenny taxi drove to the Orient Salvage Company. It was sandwiched between a school and a sewer plant. Inside the yard there were masses of broken cars in various stages of deterioration. The entrance was barred by a chain stretched between two posts; and this was guarded by a tired old Cerberus, who promptly challenged Onuma. He had seen him get out of the sixpenny taxi and lift two boxes out and carry them with obvious strain to the gate. Having formed his own views of the prospective client he affected an attitude of extreme boredom until Onuma roused him.

"Wetin?" he growled.

"Can I see the manager?"

"We no get manager here. Wetin you want?"

"I want a salvage car."

"Salvage car? No be manager you say you want?"

"Well, can I see the manager?"

The gate man departed without a word and soon came back with a small man in overalls. Both of them surveyed Onuma without much enthusiasm.

"Can I see the manager now?" asked Onuma.

"This is the engineer," said the gateman severely.

The other thin youth glanced at Onuma with reproach. He appeared to be one of those unhappy men who would dearly love to dominate but are conscious of their lack of the requisite presence.

"What do you want the manager for?" the engineer asked.

"I have told this gentleman."

"Never mind what you told this gentleman."

"I would like to hire a salvage truck."

"We are closed."

Onuma had been afraid of this, but his will to salvage his car that day was too tightly wound up and he could not allow it to be broken.

"You are closed so early?" he temporized.

But just then a brownish man of obviously oriental extraction emerged from one of the offices and asked indifferently: "What is it all about?"

"I wondered if I could hire a salvage truck."

"Of course," said the oriental who proved in fact to be the mysterious manager. "You had an accident?"

"Oh yes," said Onuma eagerly. "Thirty miles away...."

"You know you will have to pay before you take the truck?"

"Yes, all right," agreed Onuma.

The engineer was beginning to sulk away when the manager noticed him and said to Onuma: "The engineer will go with you."

The engineer said nothing, but merely turned his back boorishly and walked into his office. Onuma, although encumbered by his two bags, hurried after him. Inside the office, a poky hole cluttered with car junk, they sat in silence as if daring each other to make the first move. The uncomfortable ice was broken by a cashier who, apparently on instruction from the manager, had brought papers for Onuma to sign. Onuma turned to him with relief. The cashier, unlike his colleague the engineer, was a pleasant, clean youth in a tie. He chatted amiably while Onuma paid the cost of hiring the truck and signed papers. Meanwhile the other man, under cover of their socializing, had slipped out to attend to his own business. When, after the cashier had gone, Onuma looked out on to the open yard he saw a much beaten-up but active salvage truck waiting to go. The engineer was in the driver's seat, still in his attitude of aggrieved boredom. When he saw Onuma he indicated with a tired gesture that Onuma had better come up. A few minutes later they were on their way.

The engineer proved, much to Onuma's surprise, to be quite a loquacious fellow. The dominant theme of his conversation was the ill-treatment he had received at the hands of his employers. The owners of the salvage company were Lebanese and this fact was considered by the engineer to be an injury in itself. "Look, I have nothing against you," he told Onuma.

Onuma was glad to be reassured on this point.

"But those Lebanese, I can't stand them. Look at him," the engineer declared rhetorically. "He calls himself manager but knows nothing. All the work is in my hands. In Europe where I trained, this so called manager would never get beyond shop boy. But here, because his brother owns the company, they make him manager. Do you know how many years I trained for this job? In Europe?"

Onuma nodded to encourage him.

"Six years, five in Paris and one in London. Six years in Europe is no joke. But what do I get for it? To be placed under a Lebanese shit."

Onuma couldn't help thinking that it was the Lebanese shit who had made possible his hiring the salvage truck, but he amiably let the engineer get some of his obsessions off his chest.

"You know what I would do if I had my way?"

"What?"

"Chase them all out of the country."

"There may be the question of compensation."

"Compensation nothing, they have been sucking the blood of this country dry. We don't owe them anything."

Onuma began to warm to the oppressed man. He could see from the way the engineer handled the salvage truck that he was competent, probably a brilliant engineer. His joy in life had been dampened by a deep burden of injured merit.

At a point in the road roughly midway to Aniocha they passed a drinking place called "International Hotel". Onuma made the engineer stop and bought him a beer to cheer him up a bit. It did cheer him up to the extent that he now began to laugh and also talk very loud. All the rest of the journey he talked about his unrealized dreams, his poor pay and his European training. It was as if the sluice gate to his frustrations, which he had always kept shut was now temporarily opened. His mood was almost pleasant when he stopped in the centre of Aniocha. Onuma told him they hadn't got there yet.

The engineer's countenance clouded over. His suspicions returned.

"But you said Aniocha. I heard you," he declared.

"It is only a mile to go," said Onuma.

The engineer took time to digest this. Then at last, shrugging his shoulders with bitter resignation, he started the truck and gloomily drove on.

When they reached the spot where the Jaguar had gone over the precipice, there beside the road lay its ragged skeleton. The engineer had gone past it before stopping, and at first Onuma thought that because of the uncertain light of the oncoming dusk he had been mistaken. But when the salvage truck reversed to the spot his anguish was confirmed.

But so strong is human self-delusion that Onuma could not yet take in or believe the stark evidence lying a few yards away. With trembling hope and fear he jumped out of the truck and walked nervously to the edge of the precipice. There stood the rock which had saved the car twice but could not save it for a third time, an old rock, indifferent to all varieties of human agony. This was indeed the place. Those scraps of metal were his car.

The pathos of death was broken by the voice of the engineer.

"They cannibalized it eh? Really cleaned it up. What do we do now?"

In answer Onuma burst into agonized weeping.

The engineer took fright. He had not been at ease with this young man who had been so insistent. He had suspected the fellow right from the start. And now he was proved right. The engineer was reassured in his basic philosophy of life: "You cannot do anything with people." Accordingly he must get out quick. So turning the salvage truck round, he stepped on the gas and zoomed off.

With the departure of the truck, Onuma was overwhelmed by a deep sense of human loneliness and his tears for his beloved flowed faster. And it was his tears more than anything else that drew the crowd after him as he walked home.

Oliaku was the first to run out of the compound. When she saw the crowd and who was walking in their midst, she burst into mournful wailing.

A great many *umunna* were among the crowd which

included Magic, which goes to show how effective was the system of bush signalling which the villagers used.

Udemezue, holding a small lamp in his left hand, loomed large and solid and indestructible behind his carved doors. As soon as they saw him the crowd halted. Onuma who was leading stopped and his eyes fell. Oliaku had elaborated her crying to include invocations of dead spirits of ancestors, and a few other women were responding to her mood.

"Come in everybody," said Udemezue coolly.

"This way," said Magic, falling into his role of master of ceremonies.

"It is enough, woman," a neighbour chided Oliaku and took charge of her as well as the other women who had become helpless with tears. They were all shepherded to the women's dwellings.

Magic took charge. As the crowd filed into the obi he took Onuma aside and whispered mysteriously. Then aloud for the benefit of the others: "Leave it to me." Then he went into the hut himself, took a place and began to pick his teeth.

Onuma didn't go in with them but stood apart outside the obi. Magic roared at him: "Onuma, legend of Lagos, is this the way you welcome people into your home? What is the matter with him? Man!" he called out to Onuma who still stood there at a loss. "Man, come inside and offer hospitality in your father's house."

For answer Onuma fell down, kicked his legs and rolled about in paroxysms of grief.

There was deep silence. He appeared then to become calm, almost as if he was asleep. The people judged it wise to leave him as he was. But Magic shouted again: "Onuma Okudo, get up there and stop behaving like a child!"

Whether it was this injunction or something else nobody could say, but Onuma actually rose and stumbled dreamily to his house.

"I'll take care of him," said Magic before anybody could move, and went after Onuma.

He came back a moment later and whispered importantly to Udemezue: "He is asleep, the mother has gone to him."

Udemezue had faced this new crisis in his compound with calm. But at Magic's announcement he bestirred himself to offer customary hospitality to the crowd.

"See if there is anything in that pot, son," he said to Magic. There was a pot leaning rather tiredly by the household gods. Magic fussed around it for a while and shook his head. The rest of the crowd took the hint and politely declined the offer of palm wine.

"We know how bad the day is," they said. "But we also know that good days will come." After another short interval the relatives rose and departed. Some of the *umunna* still sat in the *obi* to give Udemezue more of their company before they dispersed to bed.

An old man had initiated small talk when they were interrupted by Onuma bursting in on them in great rage.

"Where is that engineer, the dirty rogue? He has stolen my luggage. Let me get my hands on him, the bastard!" His eyes wandered through the gathering. The people looked back at him in amazement, uncomprehending. And from there originated the legend of his madness.

PART THREE

Broken Images

1

The day promised to be Magic's own. He moved all the tools of his "occult" job into Udemezue's *obi* and all morning demonstrated their efficacy. One string painted in camwood he called "the blood of Chandu". Then there was a squeaking tube, a multi-coloured trident, feathered arrows, rows of cowries strung together, a plastic wreath, a painted cowtail whisk, beads of assorted sizes and colours, ivory keys, rings in cabbalistic shapes, antique coins. The thoroughness with which he had assembled this paraphernalia and his mad certainty of its power was impressive.

Magic had assumed responsibility for the cure of Onuma. He had come out with a diagnosis pat. Onuma was possessed by a potent spirit. Magic had not as yet identified the particular spirit, it would take a few days more of ritual.

But he could not guess how precarious his tenure of office as spiritual consultant to the Udemezue house-hold had become.

It was Oliaku who dispossessed him, though un-wittingly. Oliaku had got over the stage of helpless tears and was now setting out with formidable dry-eyed singleness of mind to plan Onuma's recovery. She first walked up to Obunagu to talk it over with the aunt, Udemezue's sister. After an initial excitement Chijioke at once sent for her favourite *dibia* and the three of them descended on the Udemezue compound.

The aunt, contemptuously ignoring the men at the *obi*, went straight to Onuma's house.

"So they have conspired against you, my own son. My own bright eagle. But they won't succeed. I'll see to that."

Onuma looked at the three people standing by his bed with resentment and said nothing.

Chijioke turned to her *dibia*. "Look at my boy," she said, "the only one we have got and they want to take him away from me."

The *dibia* shook his head mysteriously. "We will see," he said. He was a clean-limbed, effeminate-looking man who painted his eye-lashes with antimony.

She took him to the *obi*. And there she first ticked the men off.

"No evil man is going to destroy my son. I know you Aniocha people, I have no reason to be proud of you."

"The boy is going to be well, woman," said Magic impatiently.

"I know he is going to be well, no thanks to you." Having let off steam, as it were, she went and performed the ritual of greeting. Only then did she introduce and recommend the *dibia*.

Udemezue approved her choice. He knew the *dibia's* father. "Nwafo Udeozo of Obunagu, many a time he has snuffed with me in this very *obi*."

Magic also knew *dibia* Udeozo and the latter knew Magic. Neither approved of the other. The enmity broke out into the open at once. Magic served the newcomer palm wine.

"No, you have that cup," the *dibia* said.

"We are all friends here," said Magic angrily.

"I know, but have that cup."

"I tell you we are peaceable people here. We don't mean anybody any harm." Magic looked as if he was going to throw the drink at the *dibia's* face.

"It is the way we do it in our land," insisted Udeozo.

"Never mind, Ikenna, drink it," said Udemezue. Magic drank then refilled the cup and passed it on to the *dibia* who accepted this time.

"Are you reassured now?" Magic glared at his rival.

"Don't take offence," said the *dibia* wiping foam from his lips. "It is just a formality. This is strong palm wine. It tastes like the wine we had today at the railway station."

"Which railway station?" asked Magic, jealous of his authority as the much-travelled man.

"Oboli is the name."

"Oboli is not by the railway. It is a good half mile away."

"Who is disputing it? Half a mile is still by the railway station."

"I have lived at Oboli many years," asserted Magic, "and it is not by the railway station."

Udemezue cut short the rivalry by asking Udeozo whether he had found out what was the matter with Onuma. The *dibia* shook his head mysteriously in a way to suggest that he would not of course commit himself but. . . . Onuma would have to be moved over to Obunagu where he could keep an eye on him.

The suggestion was agreeable. Taking Onuma to another village would remove a source of embarrassment to Udemezue and forestall gossip.

But Magic didn't approve. "It is out of the question," he stated decisively. "To take him away from his people will make the illness worse. He must stay in familiar surroundings with his own people. I should know. I have had many such cases in Lagos, Kaura Namoda, Victoria, Cameroons – when I was in Mamfe. . . ."

Magic's assurance annoyed Udemezue and helped to confirm his decision to move Onuma if only to put the 'occult' doctor in his place.

"My son," he said to Udeozo and glancing spitefully at Magic, "he will go with you this evening. Chijioke will have a room in her house for him."

The problem was how to move Onuma or convince him that moving was necessary. But this proved easy. When he was told what was wanted of him he nodded indifferently. And that evening, dressed in trousers and his rumpled shirt, he stumbled along up to Obunagu preceded by his mother, the *dibia* and Chijioke. Udemezue stayed at home to attend to sympathizers and provide them with palm wine.

2

He came back two weeks later none the worse except for a shaven head which gave him a lost and empty look. The *dibia* had insisted on the shaving as a first step to healing. A lot of the medicines were to be applied on the scalp, he said; they would not penetrate the hair. Onuma had acquiesced in the shaving, or rather he had scarcely known about it.

They had caught him unawares at that stage where his mental faculties were stupified by the loss of his prized possession. When he recovered his bearings two days later he was furious. He refused to have any of the *dibia*'s medicine. They cajoled, the *dibia* threatened him, but Onuma flew into a rage and drove the *dibia* away with some well-aimed kicks. After that they left him alone. He stayed in the aunt's house for two weeks because he badly needed some respite to sort things out. This exercise – seeking a period of truce in life's battle – he was to find unrewarding. For instead of continuing to function and perhaps getting the better of time and circumstances, he simply allowed them to take the initiative and supress him. In life as in sports the important thing is not to win but to go on performing.

The effect of opting out for a while was that opting out soon became a way of life. Two weeks after he came home, he still seemed incapable of facing the task of living. He would lie in bed for days on end gazing at the ceiling and mumbling boorishly whenever anybody talked to him.

Udemezue was moved to wonder if he was cured, and taxed the *dibia* with his doubt. Udeozo came to Aniocha, his eyes blackened beautifully with antimony, drank palm wine, gazed at Onuma mysteriously and pronounced him well. As proof he asserted that Onuma looked fatter and fat was of course always an indication of health.

As a matter of fact Onuma had put on some weight, but it was the grossly flabby kind of weight which comes from lack of exercise. It unpleasantly affected his shapely body. There was a general deterioration of his physical shape. With his shaved head and a two weeks growth of beard he was fast losing his youthful good looks. But he didn't care any more. The fibres of his being were being eaten away one by one. The first of his values to go was a disciplined concern for cleanliness, for beauty, and therefore for life. Most of his expensive shirts had rotted in the damp air but he still wore them. There was such general uncleanliness about that a little bit more shouldn't be noticed. It was not much use trying to rise above the general condition. Instead, Onuma allowed what he considered the beastliness of village life to suck him into its whirlpool. It would be easy for him to pick up the numerous loose ends that he was creating in his life when he returned to Lagos.

3

He was beginning to look toward Lagos again, to live in the expectation of letters from Lagos. Several times a day he would visit the small postal agency which served Aniocha. The post-master, a thin irresponsible youth, answered his questions with consistent high spirits which exasperated Onuma.

"Oh yes, those Lagos letters. They are not here yet. But of course when they come I will send them to you. Ha ha!" He favoured Onuma with a broad grin.

One day Onuma caught the postal agent lounging with some other young friends in the verandah outside his office. Lying on the floor beside him were three stray envelopes.

"Any letters for me?"

"Oh yes. I was bringing them down to your house." The agent picked up the envelopes from the floor, hastily dusted them and handed them over to Onuma. Then he turned back to the conversation.

Onuma snatched the letters and there and then began to tear them open one by one. The first was from a garage and contained a bill for several months' petrol which he had bought on credit. The second was a third reminder – he had never received the second – from his insurance firm that his insurance had lapsed. Would he instruct them whether he wished to re-insure. The third letter was the most serious, and came from his employers.

The letter was written by Mr Koko. It was like Koko himself, officious, self-righteous and bombastic. He must have enjoyed writing it. The upshot of it was that Onuma had lost his job. And then followed platitudes about "abuse of trust and confidence". All of which shook Onuma less than the rider. Apparently, after soul-searching and agonizing, the company had decided to hand over Onuma's case to the police.

Onuma did not under-rate the extent of the problem he would face when he returned to Lagos, his city. Finding another job, convincing Mr Karolides, talking his way through the police, and he had to do all this robbed of the physical and psychological crutch of a car. . . . The enormity of the prospect underscored his deep-seated desire to put off action for a while.

4

Meanwhile at home itself he was day by day being made to face the stark reality of rural indigence. His money situation was reaching a critical level. He had spent most of the company money in buying spare parts for his car and paying for the salvage truck he never used. Now he was dangerously reaching the very bottom of his purse.

The village was the last place in which to be short. There was no one to turn to. Hardly anyone else in the village had any money. Onuma was struck by the scale of the villagers' indigence. When all the money in their hands was gathered at any one occasion it would not exceed a few pounds. His monthly salary could sustain the whole village for months. And yet it was from their penury that they sent their children to school, paid taxes, took the *ozo*.

As his money ran out there were hints that he had overstayed his welcome in the village: for example, encounters with a certain albino who kept an "off-licence" shop where you could actually buy cold beer. When he first came home this gentleman had literally abased himself before Onuma, allowed him to buy cartons of beer on credit with the words: "From a person of your rank one shouldn't demand money." Now, after his fall, the albino would look at him searchingly and say: "You have money?" before selling to him.

The fact was that he exasperated and puzzled the villagers. The story of his rise, decline and madness was common talk all over the ten towns. A few claimed he was cured. But if he was, why didn't he pack up and go back to Lagos? Instead he remained in the village and behaved as if he was a princeling from another world who, after a temporary set-back and given time, would rise to his old station.

There were problems also with his father. Udemezue had by now written off Onuma as a total loss and had forgotten about him. It was the only way he could bear the pain of what was to him life's major failure.

But he could not quite tolerate the idea of Onuma becoming a burden on his slender resources. One day he called him. Onuma sat on an easy chair, playing listlessly with the cloth cover.

"The farm season is on now," said Udemezue pointedly, "and we need extra hands."

"Extra hands?"

"Early tomorrow morning you will go with the labourers to the hill farm."

"So you think I am staying here?"

"But you are staying."

"Impossible. As soon as I get my things fixed up, I'll go back to Lagos. I have been going to waste here."

Udemezue said nothing for a while and then decided that he could use some self-pity himself.

"I don't know why this kind of thing should come to my house. Something has clouded the eyes of my fathers." He looked severely at the Ikenga, an important member of the *lares*. "God damn the spirit of my fathers," he said, snuffed and went out.

"Amen," said Onuma silently. "And God damn the spirit of my father."

The extent of Onuma's desperation could be gauged by his appealing to Magic, the man of all others for whom he had the most unaffected scorn. Magic looked as if he was exempt from the general village poverty. Of course he was not really a villager, his sharp practice extended the length and breadth of Nigeria.

Magic made Onuma's task more difficult by his manner of injured hostility. He had been chilly towards the Udemezue house since his curative services had been rejected. But when he had heard Onuma out he thawed somewhat. He evaded the matter of a loan but was liberal with advice on ways of making money. There was going to be a general election only a month from now. And Onuma should be able to obtain a position as an organizing secretary with a liberal salary. Magic claimed he was the General Secretary of the Party in the ten towns of the District group. And he implied that if he was treated right he might make things easy for prospective candidates. "Leave it to me. I will speak to my friend, the Honourable Chief Eze of Isu," he said.

Finally, Magic hinted that there was a money-lender at Isu and that his rate of interest was low. Onuma calmly acquiesced. In normal circumstances he would have stopped short of this humiliation, but his decision-making faculties had withered. He was inclined to go along with any suggestion so long as it saved trouble. The time for discrimination was when he got back to Lagos, a city whose pulse he could feel and understand.

Magic at first hesitated, then frowning, explained his reluctance. Onuma's father had employed him to make a spell for him and in spite of the effectiveness of the spell had refused to pay him. Magic hoped that Onuma understood that the world operates on the principle that no man works only to fill another's belly.

Onuma understood what Magic was getting at and assured him that when he received the loan the occult doctor would receive a cut of it.

"My commission is ten percent," asserted Magic firmly.

"Yes, ten percent," said Onuma contemptuously.

The contempt escaped the insensitive Magic. He led the way to Isu. But apparently the Isu money-lender did not like the look of Onuma. After a secretive whisper with Magic in the poky hole that served for his bedroom, he returned and delivered a monologue on the difficulties of the money-lending business.

Onuma, suddenly becoming angry, boasted about the powerful position that he occupied in Lagos. And besides, everybody knew that he was the son of Udemezue Okudo of Aniocha.

"How long did you stay in Lagos?" the Isu man asked.

"Fifteen years," Onuma said.

Magic and the money-lender exchanged glances.

"Well, I'll think about it and let you know."

"When?" Onuma asked furiously.

"Oh soon, soon," the man smiled evasively.

It was only later that the significance of the smile dawned on Onuma. Magic and his Isu friend did not believe he was sane.

5

Onuma felt so dispirited that he had to have some really strong drink. Fortunately the monthly dance of Isu was taking place that day. He still had a few coins in his pockets, enough to buy him entry into the dance and a few drinks. But the Isu dance was unsatisfactory. It was like a punctured bubble, the glamour had gone out of the show. It was like returning to the scene of a gorgeous spree and finding it converted into a fish market or service station.

The market mammies struggling to wedge their ample bodies through the milling crowds got on his nerves. The band was too loud. Drunken people nauseated him. The prostitutes' bored manner had lost its attraction. Onuma could see through their paint to the ravaged faces beneath.

He drifted to a quieter scene – a garish brothel on the other side of the town. He had just settled down to a beer when there was a tremendous explosion coming from the front yard. Onuma gripped his seat tight and waited. A moment later a team of roisterers trooped into the brothel. They were led by a huge man whose thunderous voice had caused the explosion. He was still going strong, shaking the building to its very foundation. He was so fat that his chest sprouted huge, flat mammae.

The group took a long bench close to a wall on which was painted a half nude picture of what to them seemed a sophisticated society girl but was in fact an incredibly self-conscious peasant. The fat man was roaring for drinks and food, and nervous waiters were running to and fro between bar to bench. He was obviously a well-known character in the brothel.

"What will you have, Danger?" the fat man roared.

Danger said he would have goat-meat.

"Service, goat-meat!" thundered the fat man.

It was brought to them in little round bowls. Fatty fell on it, dipping his hands in and cramming hunks of flesh into his huge mouth, talking all the time.

"Listen, I have known this character for forty years. Tell them about the day we first jammed."

A person of indeterminate age and sex was perched on his lap. A heavily rouged face, two bloodshot, resentful eyes, a drab over-washed frock.

"She has been at it for so long. You harlot!"

The harlot's lips spread in a mirthless smile. She prodded the mammae. This served as a kind of mating response, for the fat man jack-knifed her up with his knees and followed her to an out-house behind the lounge. A few minutes later they came back. The fat man seemed suddenly to have lost his zing. He wobbled slowly to his seat and dropped wearily into it, and avoiding the ironic glances of his friends, dipped his hands once more into the goat-meat.

But the girl stood over him menacingly.

"*Oga*, wetin now?" she asked in a voice the edges of which were frayed with impatience. The fat man didn't even look up.

"Or you wan make I tell what happen. You wan

make I tellam to the whole world. If you no take time I go shame you bad bad today."

Still not a word from the fat man. The effort at speaking was too much for him.

"Orighti, since you wan make I tell it, I go tell it. We do the ting two time and my money is ten sining. If you no pay me now now I go die here today. You no go leave here today. You go kill me before you go." Her voice was rising to an hysterical shriek.

"Have some goat-meat," the fat man was able to bring out at last. This was the most he could do for her. He had squandered his energy for her sake, and it seemed unfair to expect him to pay her money to boot.

"Sisi, have some goat-meat," he said again suddenly, without looking at her.

His casual manner drove the girl wild. For some minutes she stood over him hurling the most unprintable abuse at him. But she might have been shouting at a block of wood. Her only audience was the fat man's followers who roared encouragingly at her exotic choice of words.

The fat man went on stuffing himself until his plate was empty. Then he rose unceremoniously and rolled out followed by his friends. The woman sprang on him and hung on his shirt, calling out to the world to come and watch her being slaughtered.

"Landlord, if you are the owner of this house come and see murder," she shrieked.

The landlord emerged from nowhere, it seemed, and stood for a while smilingly admiring the scene.

"*Oga* Transport, is it well?" he said deferentially.

The fat man referred to as "*Oga* Transport" said calmly: "Never mind, landlord, she is only playing with me. She wants me to give her another one." Wit came with returning vigour.

With a guffaw the landlord took some rapid steps, prised the woman's hands from the man's shirt and held her kicking while the fat man slumped into a car, waited just long enough for his followers to jump in and zoomed noisily away.

Baulked of her prey the woman turned on the landlord but was sensible enough not to offend the man on whom her precarious living depended. She found an outlet to her passion in kicking and shrilling obscenities. But she could not maintain that level of passion for long. Eventually she sank on a chair exhausted, every now and then belching out like a diminished volcano.

At last she came back to the bar parlour and, ignoring the jeering eyes of the waiters, went and sat by Onuma who seemed to be the only man who did not revile her.

Onuma more by force of habit than anything else ordered a beer for her. She said nothing to this but gazed at him speculatively.

He looked away. There was something about her skin which he could not bear to look at. It was coming out in rashes, a skin damaged by bad food, late nights and endless abortions.

They drank in silence. After a while she kicked his legs under the table.

"Yes, what is it?" asked Onuma turning his head slightly.

"You want me for short time or for whole night?" she asked.

"Oh, never mind." Onuma shrugged impatiently.

She couldn't understand him. He wouldn't have bought her a beer if he didn't want something. Perhaps he hadn't heard her properly. She kicked his leg again.

"I say abi you wanti me for short time or for whole night?"

This was the time to depart, thought Onuma. He rose, paid for drinks and muttering a farewell to her, walked out.

She gazed at his back for a minute then shrugged her shoulders. Must be drunk or ill. He was nice though. A pity she couldn't get at him. The men who exploited her were at least men. The others, the nice ones, were either sick or women.

6

Onuma took a down-at-heels bus from the local motor-station. His travelling companions were market women from the nearby hamlets who had come to Isu to re-plenish their stock of cassava and fish. They had been delayed by the scarcity of good transport until finally they were forced to use this smoky bus which had been lying idle, disregarded, all day. There was a formidable pile of goods to load into the vehicle and this taxed to the full the ingenuity and callousness of the loaders. The driver himself, a half-naked young man with a vermin-ous cap, enjoyed slave-driving the women.

"Heh! You! Curses on your—" and he would mention some unprintable area of her body. "You can't bring that in. You want us drenched?"

"But it is only the cassava I bought yesterday. If you only knew how much I paid for it!" the woman yelled.

"Okay, bring it over here, that's right! Damn you, here! Never seen such sheep! Get moving now, we are not going to stay here all night."

The women, between nervous cries and excited laughter, fell on each other as they scrambled to bring in the rest of their loads.

"My chi! at this rate shall we get home tonight."

"My sister, how much do you say the old calabash cost?"

"Help! the car is moving . . . No! No! Driver have mercy!"

The driver in a fit of sadism had revved up the engine savagely, pretending he was about to move. When he had enjoyed enough of the women's panic he jumped down and chivvied them about once more.

At last the loads had been piled in somehow. Then the human cargo had to squeeze themselves in as best they could. Onuma found a tiny space between two anxious women, one of whom seemed to be getting into a vehicle for the first time in her life. They kept up an endless stream of talk all through the journey. One of them was complaining of the troubles she had with one of her co-wives.

"And you know, whenever my man asks her for bitter-leaf soup she says 'It's finished'. 'When do you ever have it?' he shouts. 'I don't know, but it is finished.' Finally she goes home to her father's house. And the last we hear is the accusation that I put *ogwu* in our soup to direct my husband's attention from her to me."

"She must be mad."

"You are telling me! Madness has always been in their family."

"Oh, we have passed Isu," cried the novice woman. "How fast these things move. A few moments ago we were in Mbamili and now we have gone past Isu."

"She says that all my children are not my husband's. And I reply, woman, let us go before the *Alusi* and put our fidelity to the test—"

"You ought not to be wrangling with her. Something bad may come of it."

The fare collector was going up and down, climbing over the pile of human and non-human cargo. All along the aisle he was involved in quarrels over fares.

"From Isu to my home we have always paid twopence, my son."

"Twopence! Why don't you ride free? Pay up now or I will—" He did not quite state what he was going to do. Some of the women paid. Others stuck out for a lower fare and out-talked, out-faced the collector.

On the first of his trips up and down the bus the collector had been so preoccupied with the women that he had missed out Onuma. It became therefore certain that on his return he would confront him. Onuma dipped his hand in his pocket to take the money out in advance, and then catastrophe! He had spent the last penny he had on earth in buying beer for the brothel woman.

What would he do? He calmed the panic which had been spreading through nerves, causing small beads of sweat on his forehead. There was nothing for it. He would stall the fare collector until they got to Aniocha, then he would ask him to go to his home and borrow threepence from his father, no not Udemezue, perhaps from his mother. The plan was flimsy but it might work. Or what about slapping his pockets in astonishment and claiming he had lost his purse?

"Your money? You in the suit where is your money?"

"I have already paid," said Onuma casually.

"Nonsense! Your money quick. . . . Or I will throw you out, suit and all!"

The women sitting by Onuma looked curiously at him. They knew he hadn't paid but they were not going to tell. Their sympathies were always against the lorry people.

"I have paid," insisted Onuma. Then he put up a show of anger. "This man is annoying me. If I had known that this is the way you operate this old wagon I would not have got in at all."

But this only brought into question the quality of the bus, a point on which its owners were understandably touchy. "What's the matter with him?" the driver shouted, crashing the bus to a stop and coming round to the back. "What was it he said?" He towered threateningly over Onuma.

"He wears a suit and yet can't pay threepence."

"He said something about the bus. If you don't like it why don't you go and buy a car."

"I have a car," said Onuma.

"He has a car!" The driver and his two apprentices were in stitches.

"If you knew who you have to deal with you would be more respectful."

"He has a car. A threepenny car!" – "Throw him out, the bum. Threepenny suit!"

Even the women were struck by the incongruity of the situation and joined in the laughter.

"Thow him out: Ha ha!"

But Onuma would not undergo this final humiliation, especially before the grinning women. He grasped the spring supports and held on doggedly.

"Throw him out!" shouted the driver, put on his mettle.

One person grasped him by the throat, another prised his hand from the seats. And yet a third laid a huge head against his bottom.

"*Eshobay!*" the driver cried in an ecstasy of enjoyment.

"Eee!" the others replied.

"*Eshobay!*"

"Eee!"

And together they sent him sprawling onto the tarred road. As the bus moved on, one of the conductors spat back at him.

"One of these days I will take a ride in your car. Your threepenny car!"

"I will get even with you," cried Onuma rising painfully.

"Threepenny suit!" An enormous laughter rolled away into the night.

Onuma at once built up a picture of himself as he once was, a prince in a Jaguar the laces of whose boots those servile motor people would have been unfit to loosen. But the vision was inadequate to salve the bruises on his knees and shorten the painful three-mile walk home.

7

Onuma, casting around for a weapon to break the paralysis he was in, thought he might try religion. He had been brought up a Roman Catholic but in his youth he had ceased to use religion. As he understood it, Christianity did not contribute to the three major symbols to which he had dedicated his life. It did not represent beauty, as a woman's body could be said to do. It did not suggest power as, say, Napoleon did at the height of his pride. It did not symbolize intelligence, the mastery of life through superior brain power.

Instead of these positive values it offered the negative ones of self-denial and humility. These values were contrary to his concept of himself. And they were certainly not of much use to his people. Self-denial was not much of an achievement, if you were born in circumstances under which it was inescapable. Onuma had always to remind himself that the basic reality of people born in his part of the world was represented by three words – poverty, disease, hunger. An attitude of stoicism was possibly the best response to such a hard life but it would be cruel to try to make what was obviously a heavy burden appear like a virtue. And if self-denial was hard for people who had always known it, it was harder for someone who, starting out from the grassroots of want, had got as far as the threshold of the good life; who had been taken up by a combination of the world's satans to the high pinnacle of desire and shown the immense possibilities of life.

But if intellectually he had drawn away from Christianity, emotionally he was attracted back. Especially during this period of despair. Christianity was invented by underdogs for underdogs. And Onuma had become one of the deprived of the earth. So he began to like Christianity. He was re-discovering the feelings associated with Sunday, the feeling of beginning again, the habits of fraternal communion. He began to wash his shirts again, usually on Saturdays for use on the next day. He could find nothing to iron the shirt with, but he would wear it rumpled and clean. In the absence of any other form of entertainment he looked forward to the weekly mass. He found he could listen to the long church prayers without undue strain.

And even the songs which the school choir bawled out in cracked, uneven voices had a soothing effect. But one Sunday as he came to the church he found the doors half-shut and his way barred by a stern contemptuous Tailor.

"You are late," he said sharply.

"So what?" asked Onuma.

"So what? You will have to pay a fine, that's what."

A number of school children had noted the situation from afar and, rightly gauging its true import, were racing away home. Two or three church leaders raced after them and a little while later bore in two or three kicking indignant urchins.

"Who says I am late?" asked Onuma.

Tailor forbore to comment on such a silly question but dared Onuma to get past him. Suddenly something gave way in Onuma, something long pent up in him was threatening to burst. Tailor may have read the message accurately or perhaps he had other reasons for changing his mind. But he shrugged his shoulders and let Onuma pass.

Onuma walked in, still boiling inwardly. In the church itself there was tension generated probably by the riddle of the closed doors and the whip-wielding teachers who guarded them. All through the service many an anxious school-boy's attention was riveted to the whips, and well it might be. For there was a full scale inquisition preparing. For many weeks past, attendance at church functions had been desolutory. The catechist and the teachers had been compiling a record of absentees, and that Sunday was to be the day of reckoning. As soon as Mass was over and the priest had gone, all the culprits were called up, trembling, and divided into groups. Then the catechist and the teachers set about whipping the boys. The church was soon re-echoing with the sound of cudgels and the wails of agony. Relays of "good" boys were sent into the bush to cut new whips to replace the ones which had worn out, and those victims who tried to break out, were firmly thrown back in by church vigilantes.

At last the punishment had been meted out. The church floor was littered with broken rods. A couple of half-naked urchins still danced about in pain.

The catechist sat in the midst of the church leaders known as "Committee", sweating profusely and breathing hard. The other teachers, not quite so exhausted, cleared the church of the main casualties. But they also took care to keep the door shut for there was still the trial of grown men to come. The offences varied from being absent from mass to not performing "Easter Duty". A variety of fines were levied for those offences and most of the men paid them. Those who couldn't pay were to be raided by a strong-arm group of the church and their property seized as a pledge until they paid up.

Onuma had watched the proceedings with a mixture of melancholy and impatience. He didn't think he was involved in any of it. When the Mass ended he had risen to go, but on seeing the teachers determinedly locking the door and calling back those who desired to leave, he had bided his time. Now, after the trials and whippings, he rose and made his way to the main door of the church. An angry roar pursued him.

"Onuma, son of Udemezue Okudo, where are you going? Stop him! Shall he escape us!"

Onuma turned back and saw Tailor standing in the middle of the church like an Israelite prophet predicting disaster.

"Don't let him go!" Tailor signalled furiously in the kind of urgent tone one would use when shouting "Stop, thief!"

Three young men barred Onuma's way. Onuma gauged the situation and decided it would be wiser to comply. Accordingly he walked to the "Committee" to stand his own trial. The catechist who had now recovered

from his exertions took him on. There was very little of
the unctuousness with which he had welcomed Onuma
the previous month. His manner now was threatening.
The charges were that Onuma had not come to church
on a number of Sundays; and then that he had promised
the church a gift of fifty pounds and had failed to re-
deem the pledge.

"What we want to know is: are you going to pay or
not? Are you a member of this church or are you not?"
And why hadn't Onuma made any effort to bring his
father, Udemezue into the church?

"What my father does is his business. I am not to be
held responsible for his actions."

This answer was unsatisfactory. The catechist, with a
smile of triumph, quoted passages from the Bible to
prove that anyone who let his relatives die in sin was
damned forever himself.

It looked as if the trial would end on that note but
Tailor roared out: "Where is the fifty pounds he owes
us?"

"You will get your fifty pounds and even more. As
soon as I get back to Lagos. What is fifty pounds to
me?"

This grand casualness went down rather well with
the audience.

"Nobody doubts the Okudo house," a palm-wine tap-
per said admiringly amidst noises of approval.

"I doubt him," roared Tailor. "It is all very well to
come here in a car the other day. As if a car is new to
us! The man is as empty as me. And yet he bought a
car. Yes!" he bristled.

"If it's a car that's worrying you, why don't you buy
yours?" asked Onuma.

"Was the one you rode your car? Or was it borrowed?" roared Tailor.

119

"Even borrowing a car is beyond you and your son."

"You are telling me!"

Both men stood toe to toe hurling insults at each other and gesticulating wildly; until they were calmed by the collective voice of the "Committee".

But Tailor eventually carried the day. It was agreed that property should be taken from Onuma's house to hold as a pledge until he paid fifty pounds.

"If any man comes to my house I'll knock him down," said Onuma furiously. This last threat only destroyed the slight goodwill which his offer had created: there was a large number of indignant, vindictive volunteers to go to the house and exact the pledge. Onuma preceded them. When they came he watched them menacingly as they ransacked his house and prised open his iron spring bed. The idea was to dismantle the bed and carry it away in bits. But suddenly Tailor discovered Onuma's battery-operated radio receiver.

"This will do," he cried excitedly snatching the radio receiver and running out with it.

"Bring that radio here," said Onuma running after him. They passed the gate followed by the other church people. Other curious spectators were also springing up everywhere.

"If you don't give me that radio I will knock you down," said Onuma catching up with and holding on to Tailor.

"Try it."

Onuma knocked him down.

Tailor behaved in a curious way. He lay very still, his ferocious countenance settled into an expression of dismay.

There were anxious cries from those around.

"Has he killed him?" asked an old woman.

"Of course he has."

"Give way," said the old woman taking charge. But just as she was bending down, the unpredictable Tailor surprised everybody again. He rose slowly, shook his head, glared ferociously at the crowd and holding his ear by the hand started running in the direction of Isu.

"What," said the woman angrily, "Let us look at your head."

"The police will carry you," Tailor declared. And continued running.

8

Two policemen manned the police post at Isu. They hated working on Sundays and were usually short with local people who came to report cases of assault or petty thievery. They were a sergeant and a lance-corporal. In temperament they were incompatible and there had been an element of malice on the part of the superior officer who had assigned them to the same shift. The sergeant was a drunken bully who was not above cuffing his subordinates whenever he was in the mood. The corporal, for his part, was an obstinate youth who questioned every order no matter how sober the giver was. But on this Sunday afternoon mutual feelings of boredom brought them together. The sergeant had sent the corporal to a nearby wayside shop to buy garri and stockfish. They had soaked this in water and were drinking it with obvious signs of relish. It was at this moment that Tailor, weary and incoherent with rage, rushed in.

"I want to report an assault. Assault and battery!"

The sergeant looked up with a frown: "You will wait," he said.

"He nearly killed me. I will show him what I am made off," whined Tailor.

"You took part in an affray?" asked the corporal with wan curiosity.

"He nearly killed me," shrieked Tailor.

"Is that a reason why I shouldn't finish drinking garri?" roared the sergeant. "Now you just sit down on that bench or I'll lock you up. Assault and battery indeed: pity they didn't knock your head off."

Tailor slunk to a seat and held his head in his hand in an exaggerated posture of pain.

The two officers calmly went on with their repast.

At last, replete and a little mellowed, the sergeant looked up, wiped his lips with his hand and said to Tailor: "Now then what's the matter with you?"

"He nearly killed me," shrieked Tailor again.

"Hasn't your friend a name?" cried the sergeant his temper ruffled again.

"The son of Udemezue Okudo at Aniocha."

"Oh, you come from Aniocha?"

"Yes. . . . But for my luck I would have been killed."

"And good riddance. Now, never mind about being killed. Tell us the story. Start from the beginning." The sergeant gestured menacingly.

"That's right," said Tailor. "It was the church that sent us to get his things. He had been owing us, you see." Tailor gave a long and full account of the church methods of exacting fines.

"Yes, yes, we know all that," said the sergeant. He hadn't been listening. It had just occurred to him that he could very well have delegated this chore to his subordinate. So angrily he said. "I don't understand what the blockhead is getting at – corporal take him on."

But the corporal would not. "My shift is ended." He

looked at his watch: "It is now twelve o'clock, I should be relieved by now."

"But your relief has not arrived. You will continue until he does."

"I am not responsible for my relief not arriving."

"You will take down this man's statement, sir."

"I will not, sir."

"Corporal, this is an order."

"It is not an order. My shift is over and nobody is going to order me about in my own time."

"Very well, I'll make a note of this," said the sergeant. He extracted a pen from behind his ear and began to scribble angrily on a piece of paper. After a while he looked up to see if this had the desired effect. It hadn't. He filed his pen back to his ears, took a notebook and stumped out. The corporal turned sullenly to Tailor:

"You took part in an affray?"

Tailor repeated that the son of Udemezue Okudo had knocked him down.

"He came up to you and knocked you down just like that?"

Tailor once again told his story.

"I see," said the corporal. "You took part in an affray." The corporal made a quick and rapid entry in his notebook and got Tailor to make a mark with his thumb. Then he thought for a moment: "Where did you say that this assailant lives?"

"The son of Ozo Udemezue Okudo of Aniocha."

The corporal considered again. If he took the case on as he was required to do he would have to ride out five miles, in his own spare time too. No, he would wait and hand the case to his relief. But the relief did not turn up. Eventually, after an hour, the corporal decided that he would leave a note of "explanation" for him.

He locked up Tailor in a small cell close to the police post. Just as he was about to leave, the relief came and was profuse with apologies, but the corporal was too anxious to get away to have time for reprimand.

"A case of affray," he said. "One of the parties is in the cell. You may have to ride out to apprehend the other."

"Okedoky." But when the new officer read the note it seemed to him that the corporal who started the job should be the one to complete it. The case would wait till the next morning. It wouldn't do the man who was locked up much harm to have a day's cool-off.

A few moments later the sergeant looked in, in a fairly cheerful mood. He had just had a quick one at the local pub.

"Everything okay, constable?"

"Yes sir. One case of affray. We've seen to it."

"Very good. . . . I'll be with you soon."

"Yes sir."

The next morning the recalcitrant corporal appeared in Aniocha disguised in plain clothes and asked to be directed to one Ozo Udemezue Okudo. The peasants who sat on the *ogwe* at once connected the request to the incident of the previous day which had, of course, become common property. They recognized the policeman for what he was and treated him accordingly to the village code by which officers of the law were to be misled, misinformed and generally prevented from getting at people.

"Udemezue Okudo?" said somebody from the crowd; "He is not a man of this town."

"There is such a name in Obunagu I think," added another helpfully. "His eldest son has a big three-floor house."

The corporal understood that he could glean no information from these people and departed quietly. Eventually an unsuspecting farmer led him to Udemezue's house.

Udemezue was alone at home. The corporal saw at once that he had to deal with a man of substance, and proceeded with caution. As far as he was concerned all he wanted was to be given a rewarding excuse for not proceeding with the case. Accordingly he was a little apologetic and round-about in explaining to Udemezue.

But to his surprise the old man seemed to know all about the case and to have come to his own conclusion about it: as soon as the policeman made an end he called out loudly for Onuma. And when he came into the obi Udemezue passed him on to the policeman with a relinquishing gesture.

Onuma recognized the corporal. It was the gentleman to whom he had reported the cannibalization of his Jaguar. Since then he had been to the police post three times and on each occasion they had always told him that the corporal in charge "was not here today". Onuma, meeting him again, teased him with his curious absenteeism.

The corporal was put off his balance and became angry. He was there to accuse, not to be accused. But Onuma's directness over-awed him and after shying and squirming he said unconvincingly:

"We are after the thief or the suspect. I think his name is Chuks. They tell us he has run to the north but we will catch up with him, never mind."

"Fat chance," thought Onuma.

The corporal felt more at ease in dealing with a man of his own age and possibly mental outlook. He took Onuma aside and said with professional briskness: "You are wanted at the police station. You took part in an affray."

Onuma was a little shaken and the policeman, seeing this, pressed home his advantage. "The other party has been locked up." He paused and waited for Onuma's next move. But the latter's reaction was to rail against Tailor and exonerate himself.

"Well, you had better come with me to the police station."

Onuma was taken away in full view of virtually the whole of Aniocha.

At the police station the corporal reported to the sergeant.

"A case of affray, sir. This is the other party."

"Lock him up, corporal."

"I was going to, sir." The corporal had held out to the last a chance for Onuma to buy himself free. When it looked as if the latter was incapable he lost patience with him and was quite summary in locking him up.

9

The case came up at Isu before a customary court constituted of family heads from the nearby towns, and a chairman. This last was a big man who wore regal robes and a tinsel crown. He called himself Eze – king – of Isu and had appropriated to himself a wide range of royal ceremonial from many customs. He enjoyed vast authority in the ten towns, based on his astute grasp of a variety of political strings. He was one of the first people to see the potential advantage in an alliance between politicians and natural or even self-made royalty. So he proclaimed himself king and designed royal robes.

And when at the onset of Independence ministerial government was introduced to the country, the Eze won a place in the cabinet. In doing so he not only enhanced his personal standing but added lustre to the ten towns by giving them a vicarious share in the romance and profits of rule. From that time onwards the district was very much his to do as he liked with; he was not only the Eze of Isu town but also of the district group. He could build a post office in a compliant village and remove it from a hostile one: other politicians stood against him at great peril, though of course this did not prevent them from trying.

The chairmanship of the customary court was one of his numerous sidelines. He usually arrived late, and with a retinue of staff carrying Ozo tokens. He would sit on a make-shift throne in judicious silence while the other members of the panel did the questioning and arguing.

When it came to Onuma's case the other judges, too, had little to say and the prosecution of the case was left to the corporal. The corporal said it was a case of affray.

"It was not a case of affray," said Onuma.

"Keep quiet," said one of the judges. "You think you know more than the policeman?"

The corporal confirmed that it was a case of affray.

"Is that all?" said the Eze, turning from the attendant who had been swivelling a feather fan at him.

That was all.

Well, what had the fellows to say before he sent them to prison?

Tailor pleaded the old custom by which the church exacted tribute from its members. This was directed at the Eze. Tailor knew that the "king" made a great show of his concern for the church and had on many occasions made judicious grants to the missions. And it is possible that this fact did influence his decision, for Tailor got off with a five-pounds fine while Onuma was to go to prison for two months.

But just as the two culprits were about to be taken away, one of the judges said as an after-thought: "Is he not the son of Udemezue Okudo?"

"Who?" said the Eze sharply.

"The young man."

"Udemezue Okudo of Aniocha?" asked the Eze rhetorically. He bent a concentrated, speculative look at the speaker.

"Order! Order" roared the policeman in anticipation of a statement from the great man.

"Constable, call those fellows back."

Onuma and Tailor were led back to the dock.

"You are the son of Udemezue Okudo of Aniocha?" asked the Eze sternly.

Onuma said that he was.

"And how do you think your father would feel if I sent you to prison?"

Onuma knew how his father would feel but thought it wise to keep silent.

"I have a good mind to double your sentence as an example to others. You young people have no respect for law or for yourself."

The Eze gave a long homily on the failings of the young and ended with "but for the fact that you are the son of a respected elder I would have. . . ." He didn't complete the threat.

"Take him away from my sight."

One of the attendants understood what was wanted of him, led Onuma out and released him.

"And you," said the Eze sternly to Tailor, "have you paid your fine?"

"I was in the service of the church, my lord," cried Tailor.

"Well, go and pay that fine and don't let me see you here again in my court. Go on, out with you."

Tailor was seized by a policeman and locked up for three months until somebody remembered.

As he was making his way home Onuma was accosted by a mournful looking individual.

"Are you the fellow?" asked the latter.

"Which?" asked Onuma suspiciously. He was in no mood for puzzles.

His interlocutor made a gesture which implied "none of my business", and said: "You had better come to see the Eze."

Onuma followed a little apprehensively to an apartment adjoining the court which magistrates used as their chambers.

The Eze sat in state surrounded by a large number of litigants. At that moment he was listening patiently to one of them, a farmer of Isu.

"Your honour said that she was to return to me but has she? And her people would not let me have the bride price."

"Go to them and tell them that I say she should return to you."

"We have gone several times but they have no ears to listen."

"Tell them I said."

"Yes your honour. . . ."

"Take him away," ordered the Eze with a sign to the two men who stood by his side. The farmer was dragged off protesting at the top of his voice.

Then the Eze glanced for a moment at Onuma and turned away quickly.

"This is the man," said Onuma's companion to the Eze.

The Eze, without looking up, waved them away. "Go and talk it over between yourselves," he said.

As they stood outside once again the other man said to Onuma: "You should come to the Eze's place at Isu. You know the Eze's place at Isu?"

"Yes. But what is it all about?"

"You just come, that's all," and he walked dolefully away.

Onuma returned home choking with rage. And the cool look his father turned on him only exasperated him the more.

"I could have gone to prison and nobody raised a finger. It is inhuman."

"The whole town is talking about it," said Udemezue bitterly. "The son of the Okudo house, being locked up like a common thief. I didn't think I would live to see the day."

"And what about me, do you think I enjoyed the locking up?"

"Perhaps you should really get out of our town. It doesn't matter where you go as long as you get out."

"I am getting to Lagos any day now. You wait and see."

Udemezue snuffed and relapsed into his attitude of stern patience.

10

Because of the impending general election, politics were very much in the air, and as Magic had already suggested, they might well offer Onuma a way of reviving his fortunes. As a vehicle of access to property and wealth political activity provided unrivalled prospects of instant success. In politics more than any other form of employment you could be a pauper today, a fat tycoon tomorrow. To begin to function again as a full person Onuma felt he had to regain the prestigious height accorded him by the Jaguar. Nothing less than that was worth fighting for. In fact, this was the main explanation for his passive lethargy. He would much rather coast through the squalor and indigence of the village than waste his energy fighting for anything less than a Jaguar. But if he went into politics? Might it not prove to be a game tailored for his talents? Accordingly he began to look forward to seeing the Eze. He was not unaware of what the old charlatan stood for, but his situation was desperate and he had passed the stage of squeamishness over methods.

11

In his home the Eze seemed to abandon the sphinx-like taciturnity which he presented to the world. Dressed in well-worn sleeveless shirt and wrapper he sat on a long sofa. Servants brought him various dishes in succession. He would sample each and pass it on, talking all the time. But whatever mood he was in his massive face was consistently expressionless.

The "Palace" was a happy blend of the two traditions of building which were known in the ten towns. On the one hand it had a long large hall equivalent to an *obi*, with carved panels and a raised structure at the end to support the *lares*. On the other hand there were a number of adjoining sittingrooms and bedrooms. The whole structure was roofed with corrugated iron.

When Onuma went to pay his call the Eze welcomed him graciously.

"You are the son of Udemezue Okudo? We grew up together, I lived at Aniocha when I was young."

The other Isu men who sat around the Eze also knew Udemezue and there was general talk about his exploits when he was young. . . .

"Go and see my secretary, Kabu-Kabu. He will explain everything to you." The Eze waved towards one of the adjoining rooms.

Kabu-Kabu, the secretary, proved to be the mournful individual who had accosted Onuma the previous day. He was seated behind a massive table, his head buried in a pile of accounts. Beside him stood a boy who was referring to a list pinned to a standing wooden board. The boy read aloud from the list, mostly names of the ten towns, and the secretary made notes in a book.

"Uruoji: fifty elders at five shillings each: that will be twelve pounds ten shillings. . . . Obunagu: one hundred elders, twenty five pounds. . . . Mbamili. . . . Aniocha. . . ."

"That will do. . . . What about money for the police and magistrates . . ."

"Police," read out the boy. "An inspector receives five pounds, sergeants one pound, ordinary constables ten shillings."

"Too much," said the Secretary decidedly. "After all, what did they do during the last election but stand around and let people opposed to us vote? And our own voters could not get in to vote more than two or three times apiece. Money given to the police is money wasted. Cut down their allowance to five shillings."

132

"Yes sir. Three inspectors, ten sergeants, twenty constables. . . ."

"And the magistrates?"

"Magistrates: I don't find them included here. . . ."

"Look lower down."

"Oh yes: magistrates ten pounds each. . . ."

They were so engrossed in their job that they seemed unaware of Onuma's presence. But at this juncture the Secretary looked up, waved Onuma to a seat and continued to work.

"What is the vote for marijuana, boy?"

"An ounce a day for every bodyguard. And we have twenty-five."

"That's a fortune gone on marijuana alone," complained Kabu-Kabu, noting down the figure in his book. He looked up again and favoured Onuma with an impersonal faraway look. . . .

"What was it they said you did in Lagos?"

"I was a Public Relations Manager."

"We know all about you." He went on to give a graphic account of Onuma's career. "And now you are without a job. That's why we are employing you for the election."

He smiled with only his teeth.

Onuma wondered from where Kabu-Kabu received all this information. The man was a crook, but you couldn't help being impressed by some gnarled, enduring quality in him. It was easy to see that his doleful manner concealed sharpness, even ruthlessness. Taking it for granted that Onuma had accepted his offer he asked suddenly: "Do you smoke?"

Onuma understood, of course, that the smoke referred to was not tobacco. He shook his head.

"That's one ounce of wee-wee a day saved," said Kabu-Kabu, almost regretfully. He buried his head once

133

more in his books. Finally he said: "You will come here every other day to be given your assignments. Meanwhile you could travel about the ten towns and keep your ears open. A bicycle will be provided for you and later perhaps. . . ." He did not conclude but Onuma guessed what was left unsaid: "A car". Kabu-Kabu would not commit himself so early. Onuma was also to receive a salary and the Secretary named a figure which, set against Onuma's destitution, was quite attractive.

"I shall now give you a bicycle," said Kabu-Kabu, rising wearily.

As they were passing out, the Eze called out: "Have both of you tallied?"

"We are working at it," said Kabu-Kabu miserably.

"True? and, young man, tell Udemezue for me that it is long since I drank his palm wine."

"Yes, sir," said Onuma.

"That's right."

Kabu-Kabu took him to an outhouse, and from there selected a Raleigh bicycle from among a dozen gleaming models that leaned on the wall, made a careful note of the chassis number, handed it to Onuma, and turned back with studied casualness.

Onuma had a feeling of functioning again, even if the function was only that of Public Relations – or in Nigerian political euphemism a "propaganda secretary" – to a crook.

12

Magic was the first to congratulate Onuma on his new job. It was the main source of Magic's strength that he seemed to know so many things even before they happened. "You must join the Party," he said.

"But I am a member of the Party," Onuma replied.

"When you were in Lagos? That's a different thing. You have to register with us anew. Obtain a party card." And from the way Magic said this it was clear that the obtaining of this card depended very much on Magic's personal pleasure. His activities in the next few days certainly suggested that he was the pivot of political activity in Aniocha. Two years previously Magic had wangled a position as an honorary gong-striker of the town. And now he used the gong to further his political interest. That night he walked up and down the village announcing that there would be a meeting of "the Party" the next day in the village hall.

"The Party", of course, was the Nigerian People's Union. It was taken for granted that everybody would understand it to be so. It was the only party that existed. Nobody dared form a new party. To stand out in opposition to the Party amounted to expressing lack of faith in the destiny of the race.

The possibility of being overshadowed in the Party at Aniocha was not lost on Magic. That night, when the NPU, Aniocha branch met at the town hall, he worked hard to isolate Onuma. He gave him none of his practised smiles. He was short and hostile whenever their paths crossed. The other members of the branch were a stolid bricklayer who, it was reputed, had once worked in the Cameroons; a Mr Augustine – the "Mr" being a mark of superior talent – a former prison warder now turned medicine-man; and the albino who kept the off-licence drinks shop. These three and Magic had something in common in that they had all at one time or another been exposed to the outside world and thereby formed a link between Aniocha and civilization.

Magic, after glancing grimly at Onuma, raised the question of subscriptions which should serve as both enrolment fee and assurance of continued membership.

"How many people here have paid their subscriptions?"

The albino dug the bricklayer at the ribs: "Man, tell us, you are the Treasurer."

The bricklayer had been snuffing placidly and looked up with distaste.

"What is it?" he asked, squinting at the albino.

"Read us the names of the debtors," said Magic.

"Names?" the bricklayer laughed. "Nobody has ever paid. Have you ever paid?" he leered maliciously at Magic.

"That's because you don't come to ask," said Magic hastily. "All of us here are above ten shillings, what!"

"Speak for yourself," said the albino with a tremendous laugh. "If I always had ten shillings I would say goodbye to hunger."

Then Magic tried another line of attack. He described, for the benefit of Onuma perhaps, the troubles they had had building up the party in Aniocha. Now it was only fair that they should reap the full benefits of their patient efforts. But it appeared that somebody was going to frustrate their harvest. Somebody had gone to Isu and eaten the money given out by the Eze and intended for all the people of Aniocha.

This report touched raw nerves. Passions were up at once. The men looked angrily at one another.

"Who was the man?" asked the albino truculently.

"Ha!" hissed Mr Augustine disgustedly. "It is always the way of Aniocha. The monkey does the dirty work while the baboon does the eating."

The incident tailed off into recriminations of a general

nature. Magic had not enough evidence to make a specific charge.

Onuma got rid of Magic simply by declaring that he had been nominated chairman of the local branch by Eze.

Magic laughed incredulously. "So that is the way these things are done nowadays. We work and toil here for nothing and they think they can order us about. . . . Well go and tell your Eze. . . ."

The albino had been staring at Magic while he made this speech. At last, unable to contain himself any more he fell on the rebel: "You have come again. What do you know about the Party? Are you the Eze? If the Eze wants to make this young man sheaman who are you to say no? . . . Do you know book? Have you been to univaiti? Are you not a village blockhead like all of us?"

"I am not a village blockhead. You mistake the man you are talking with."

"Oh yes, we know all about your travels but you are still a yokel, so there!"

Mr Augustine, who had been snuffing through the altercation, pushed the last thumbful of snuff into his nostrils and in between sighs of enjoyment gave his own verdict: "Young man, sheaman, I greet you. . . . If Magic wants his own sheaman he can have one but the Eze's choice is good enough for me. Ha ha!"

Magic, seeing which way the wind was blowing, hastily beat a retreat.

"I didn't say this young man is not our chairman. How can I question the Eze's order? You all know me that I have been loyal to the Party all my life. Just tell Magic what there is to do and it is done!"

He indicated his good will by stretching his hand for

a shake but Onuma decided he should be kept in his place and ignored the proferred hand.

The albino had lost interest in the subject and was speculating in undertones about some other candidate who was putting himself up in opposition to the Eze.

"It is Ikpa, isn't it?" asked Mr Augustine.

"Yes," agreed the albino. "Mad Ikpa, that was what we used to call him from childhood. He is still as mad as ever. For who else but a mad man would challenge the Eze?"

"But has he money? He can be as mad as he likes so long as he has money. That is all we are interested in. Some candidates are all words, words and no deeds. When it comes to making good on their words they collapse."

"He has money all right. . . . I hear he looted some bank in the North."

"Oh, that's good," said Mr Augustine. "Somebody has to go and collect our share."

"The chairman and I," said Magic.

Nobody contested this so the suggestion stuck.

13

Onuma was surprised to learn that the Eze's opponent was Ikpa of Obunagu, his first cousin on the mother's side, son of her sister, Adu. It was not only Onuma to whom the news was sudden, for Ikpa had kept his intentions to himself until the last moment and then suddenly thrust his way into the forefront of the contest. He was fighting on religious issues. Having made the Eze out as a Protestant he hoped to alienate him from the strong Catholic solidarity of the ten towns.

Ikpa had been away from the ten towns for almost as long as Onuma could remember and had come back only six months before the election. It was astonishing how much he achieved within that short time. First he got himself made a chief; then he bought a Mercedes with a melodious hooter and the inevitable party flag struck on its bonnet. Then, by certain calculated gifts to the Christian missions, he created a legend for open-handedness. He too was aiming, like the Eze, to reach back to a legendary period of opulence. Far from discrediting him, this would enhance his position. The people liked their leaders to start out rich. A man who sought their approval did not come with the sack-cloth of humility. He must not just be wealthy but must appear to be so.

Ikpa's status emblems included many wives – he actually married four when he returned to Obunagu, to the consternation of his first wife who had lived happily with him for twenty years. Then a palace had to be built and in building it, Ikpa, or rather Chief Ikpa, aimed at a show-piece rather than a purely utilitarian dwelling. It was of four floors sparkling with vivid glass and raving red blinds. The top three floors were virtually empty. Ikpa lived on the ground floor which he had designed to be a cross between a traditional *obi* and a village hall. Praise singers were then attached to the household and in the true tradition of grand seignorial hospitality there was always palm wine to be had in the *obi*. Onuma's first thought when he saw all this was to wonder how long it was going to last.

It seemed incredible that Ikpa should go to such lengths for an election which everybody except himself knew he had not the slightest chance of winning.

On the other hand Ikpa really did believe he was going to win. He had no doubts about that at all.

Onuma, although he could accurately assess the folly of Ikpa's decision, envied him the directness and positiveness of his action. It seemed such a contrast to his own recent indecisiveness.

When Onuma arrived at Ikpa's compound he first went to see his aunt, Adu. She sat on the raised mud bed of her home. Ikpa had covered her hut with corrugated iron but had had the sense to leave the rest of the traditional mud structure as it had always been. Meeting the aunt was for Onuma like a second homecoming. His boyhood had alternated between Adu and his mother. Adu was the elder sister but both women were astonishingly alike, the same placidity of temper, the same blind unquestioning patience. She welcomed him with her calm smile which always suggested that you had been sitting with her for ages and that she had always accepted and understood you. Onuma had never met anybody who gave him the same impression of hidden strength.

The junior wives, that is the new wives of Ikpa who lived closely with their mother-in-law, expressed their welcome more noisily.

"You will take me back to Lagos?" one asked.

"I already have a wife, you should know that."

"Which one, the one from Aniocha, or the one from Mbamili, or the one who lives in Isu?"

"The only one that matters."

"Does she give you good bitter-leaf soup?"

"She can feed me all night if I want it."

When Onuma returned to the fourth floor of the palace, he found Magic and a few other Obunagu men laughing deferentially at a joke Ikpa had made. Ikpa, dressed in embroidered robes, with a gold-lined, tassled cap was basking in the glow of the peasant' deference. Beside his seat were arranged elephant tusks and a gold-plated ozo staff, all apparently for effect; Ikpa had not yet taken the ozo.

The showy performance could have been incongruous, but for the assurance with which Ikpa carried it off. He nodded at Onuma with regal condescension and Onuma, not caring for that type of welcome, walked boldly up to him and shook hands.

"Like an Aniocha man," said Ikpa, shaking hands gravely. His audience took the cue and laughed.

Onuma did not take offence because he saw Ikpa as nothing more than an actor and a court jester at that. He decided to get into the spirit of the clowning.

"Serve us the hot drink," Ikpa ordered his servants. They dug out from a carved bureau a fresh bottle of scotch whisky with little glasses and passed these around.

"Now where are the musicians?" ordered Ikpa.

There were half a dozen of the praise-singers at one end of the room. They struck up. Onuma knew the leader, a famed artiste, who had lived his art for almost fifty years. He had aged a great deal but not his rust-sharp, palm-wine coloured voice which still retained its grace and utter sincerity.

Ikpa was full of the election. He talked above the music, bragged about his imminent success. "The whole of Obunagu is behind me."

"Very true," shouted a peasant and danced about the room both in deference to Ikpa and in response to the music.

"We will drag the Eze's face in the mud. Aniocha, Mbamili, Isu all are with me."

This too elicited a praise name from another boisterous group.

Suddenly something seemed to occur to Ikpa. "Come

this way, cousin," he ordered, seizing Onuma by the arm and forcing him to one of the corridors of the flat.

"They tell me you work with that rogue, the Eze," he said sharply.

"I didn't know you were contesting."

"Well, now you know. And you must leave him at once. He is the greatest criminal of these parts and we are going to call him to account. He is due for the greatest disgrace of his life. But of course," Ikpa went on after a moment's thought, "it might be a good idea for you to stay with him and pass me news of what he does."

"But he is my employer," Onuma protested. "He pays me salary."

"Never mind about salary," said Ikpa brushing aside this intrusion of Onuma's personal expectations into the more cosmic affair of politics. "You just do as I say. Pretend to work with him. Keep your ears open and send me word about once a week." And before Onuma could utter another word he started him walking down the corridor to a room which served as an office. It was crowded with people who all seemed to be excitedly counting money. Ikpa elbowed his way to a table where the paymaster sat.

"This is my brother," he said introducing Onuma. "He is from Aniocha."

"We are from Aniocha," said Magic, springing up from nowhere, it seemed.

Onuma gave him a scorching look.

"He will receive the money for Aniocha," said Ikpa starting out. But when he reached the door he turned back to say: "Tell your mother I haven't seen her for long."

The secretary, a lean bespectacled young man, looked

at Onuma with respect: "How many elders are there in Aniocha?" he asked.

"Five hundred," said Magic quickly.

"What!" cried the secretary, turning on Magic. "Two years ago, according to the count, we had two hundred. And I know since then half of them have died. How could you have doubled them?"

"There are five hundred," persisted Magic. "Are there not five hundred?" he appealed to Onuma.

"You will receive money for two hundred," said the secretary, "at the rate of ten shillings for each elder: that would be one hundred pounds."

He scooped currency notes from a basket, counted out a hundred and handed it to Onuma but Magic got in first, took the money, and counted it meticulously.

"You will probably eat it all," said the secretary cynically. "I don't trust you agents."

Magic replied with a non-commital smile and continued counting. On his third count Onuma snatched the money from him and put it into his own pocket.

Then he went to bid Chief Ikpa goodbye and found him toasting the spirit of his father to the accompaniment of *ozala* trumpet. He stopped, alert, when he saw Onuma and walked towards him.

"I'll drive you home," he said, and led them to a lodge in front of the house. A uniformed lodge keeper who had been dozing sprang up and saluted.

"Ask the driver to get the car round," Ikpa ordered.

"Yes, sir."

A few moments later a uniformed driver parked a huge luxury Mercedes beside them, tumbled out and opened the doors. "Get in," ordered Ikpa. And as the monster nosed its way through the golden-green twilight the owner demonstrated its mechanics and conveniences. "Does any of you smoke?" he asked. "Never mind. Here. . . ." He pressed a button and a concealed cigarette container presented a selection of luxurious cigarettes. Ikpa took one and caused the rest to disappear. "Then after you have smoked," he pressed another button and with a flash of opal a golden ash-tray yawned through the solid velvet upholstery of the seat.

Finally the radio: "Tune the radio, driver."

"Yes, sir."

But none of the stations played the kind of music Ikpa liked and he roughly ordered them to be silenced. There were other wonders such as the air-conditioner, a concealed dinner set, a bar. Magic was suitably rapturous and egged the proud owner to more demonstrations.

"I was going to install a bar in my Jaguar," said Onuma suddenly.

"You had a Jaguar?" said Chief Ikpa incredulously, in the tone Baalam would have used if his ass had boasted of its vocal acquisitions.

Onuma's ill-advised statement brought to the surface a personal rivalry between him and Chief Ikpa which had been latent through their encounters. Chief Ikpa was keenly aware of Onuma's advantage in education and sophistication and sought to counter it with superior material possessions. For him to maintain his self-esteem, it was necessary that Onuma should yield ground to him in that respect.

Onuma, quickly perceiving the man's dilemma, hastened to reassure him: "Had a Jaguar. But it has since gone to pieces."

Chief Ikpa greeted the news with a triumphant smile.

They got to Aniocha in the rust-coloured gloaming and Ikpa awakened the drowsy town with a burst of his melodious hooter. This was to be the Aniocha people's first experience of the "singing car" which was to feature so ubiquitously in the coming contest. Magic tried by fussy obeisance to convey his profound pleasure at the ride, but Chief Ikpa had no more time for him. He was now intent on seeing Onuma's mother. "Call our daughter," he ordered. She came happily. Ikpa had always been her favourite nephew.

"Mother, your son has fallen into an *alu*. Why did you let him?"

"Which *alu*? talk straight, boy. Why can't you talk straight," she smiled.

"Your son has become a member of the Eze of Isu's gang. But I have saved him from them. Now he belongs to me."

"Of course he belongs to you," said Oliaku with firm conviction.

"That's what I mean, mother." And without another word he snapped his fingers to the driver and the car slid away.

Two other members of the NPU Home branch, the albino and the bricklayer, were waiting for Onuma at his house.

"Did our man play up?" asked the albino.

"You should ask Magic."

They asked Magic.

"Did Chief Ikpa offer us any *cola* or did he not. And no Aniocha tricks, please."

Magic winked conspiratorially at Onuma and answered: "He gave us money but that was for the elders. We are not supposed to eat it."

"We know all about that," snarled the bricklayer. "The question is, how much?"

Another nod from Magic indicating "Don't tell them!"

"I can't see really what business of yours it is," Onuma said.

His apparent toughness cowed the two men. The albino shrunk a little into himself. The bricklayer was apologetic.

"We know he is your brother and therefore you have the right to do what you like with whatever he gave you. But look at us poor and unfortunate, can you send us away empty-handed? It won't be like an Okudo to do such a thing. Our people say that the hawk shall perch and the eagle shall perch, whichever says to the other don't perch let its wings break." The speech was embellished with three other folksy proverbs.

Magic indicated by his manner and several sly gestures that he was all for holding out against the appeals.

But Onuma calculated otherwise. He went into his bedroom and soon returned with a bundle of currency notes. He counted and gave five pounds to every one of the three men. Magic demurred at accepting his but when Onuma threatened to withdraw the offer he hastily grabbed it. The gratitude of the albino and the bricklayer was abject. They were unused to handling so much money, which probably represented half a year's income.

First the albino performed the ritual of *cola* over the money. Then the bricklayer thanked Onuma profusely.

"Sheaman, you have done well by us. This *cola* that you have given us will multiply a hundredfold in your bag. It is God who brought you to stay here a while with us. We bow our knees and thank him, for your stay has been fruitful. Thank you Sheaman. Thank you."

They finally took their leave, bowing deeply and

snuffing happily. Only Magic remained facing Onuma with a bright, expectant expression.

"Those men are just yokels," hẹ said.

Onuma pretended drowsiness as a way of sending him off. But Magic was persistent.

"What happens now?" he asked Onuma.

"How do you mean, what happens?"

"Well, the money your brother gave you."

"That is money really meant for the elders."

"Yes, we know about that."

"I thought you were urging me not to break the money meant for the elders," said Onuma.

"Well, it was wrong to break it before these village yokels."

"Would it be right to meet again and recall all money?"

"No, no," said Magic hastily. "I am not blaming you for anything, after all it is your cousin's money and you have every right to do whatever you like with it. Have you anything else you want me to do, sheaman?"

Onuma faked a snore which effectively put an end to further palaver.

14

When next Onuma visited the Eze he was inadvertently a participant in a deadly confrontation between him and Ikpa. Ikpa had come to the home of the Eze to beard him in his den, as it were. Eze, taking charge of operations from the top of the landing, was giving directions in an unusually excited voice.

"The first man who climbs my walls is to be shot. Is that not so?"

"Of course," said his doleful second-in-command; Kabu-Kabu.

As Onuma came up the chief looked at him suspiciously. Apparently he could not quite place him. But after a short moment he seemed to know him again. "This is the man of Aniocha?"

"Yes, sir," replied Kabu-Kabu.

"Get him a gun."

Kabu-Kabu went into the house and soon returned with an automatic gun which he handed over.

"You will need it this evening, I think," the Eze said. A chorus of war-like songs floated over the outer walls and seemed to assail the bastion of the Eze.

> Who wants to go to Hell?
> Who wants to go with the Devil?
> Let him go with the Eze.
> Who wants to go to Heaven?
> Who wants to eat life?
> Let him go with Chief Ikpa.

Then followed the rousing refrain:

> Give us Chief Ikpa
> In life or death
> We will go with Chief Ikpa.

"They will go to death with him this evening," remarked the Eze grimly.

Onuma, perplexed by the sudden turn of events, went into the house. And there he saw many of the Eze's toughs going in and out of a room marked "private". Driven by curiosity, he made his way there but at the threshold of the door he was stopped by a tall sinister-looking young man.

"What do you want?" the man asked menacingly.

"I belong here."

"Indeed," said the other fellow sarcastically.

"It is well, Gorilla," said Kabu-Kabu coming up and intervening. "He is a new man."

"When did he join us?" asked Gorilla, his suspicions still unsatisfied.

"The Eze took him on."

Gorilla grunted.

Onuma went into the room. Most of the bodyguard were seated in a semi-circle furtively smoking marijuana. Some of them, their eyes closed, were just feeling the first effect of the weed. Others, with inane smiles and weary gestures, had passed the last stages of enjoyment.

"Had your ounce?" said an individual sprawling in a corner who seemed to be the dispenser of the "smoke".

"I don't smoke," replied Onuma.

"He doesn't smoke! Several of them rushed to take his share. "He doesn't smoke," they cried together. But the dispenser was very meticulous. "One ounce a man, that's what the chief says."

As Onuma came out of the room Gorilla accosted him again.

"You've had your smoke?"

"I don't smoke."

"Is this a joke?" growled Gorilla.

"I tell you I don't smoke."

"Why then did you go in there?"

"To load my gun."

"It was already loaded, but you had no smoke?"

"No."

Gorilla continued to glare at him: Onuma was to get used to him and his unwavering look. Gorilla was the leader of the heavies. And what gave him an edge over the rest of them was a certain animal courage coupled with a complete disregard for life, his own or other people's.

The besiegers had broken off, their songs had now tailed to an end. The Eze rang a bell and all the heavies tumbled into a truck parked in front of the house and stocked with guns, knives and cudgels. There was also a Volkswagen car alongside.

Onuma was to drive with Kabu-Kabu in the Volkswagen.

There was a slight commotion near the truck. One of the men had sat in the front seat beside the driver.

Gorilla was standing over him and gazing at him fixedly, his body quivering. The front seat had by sacred custom become Gorilla's privilege. Very few of the other thugs would intrude on it – the offender had taken the seat more out of intoxicated oversight than a wish to challenge Gorilla's authority.

The others, with cries of fear, carried the offender out of the front seat and heaved him into the back. Then they set about trying to mollify Gorilla. But he would not be mollified. Shrugging his shoulders, he walked away and stood beside the outer wall, brooding. There was dead stillness. Nobody knew what he would do. It was like watching a big cat making up his mind to charge. At last Gorilla walked back. There were tears in his eyes. He had been thwarted of his need for violence and tears were the only outlet left.

The Eze had watched the incident and had wisely refrained from comment. He knew that a word from him might very well serve as the spark to set ablaze an inflammable situation. At last, when they had calmed down, he gave them final instructions.

"They will soon come by here. And you are to follow them. Chief Ikpa in his car and his people in a tip-lorry. I don't want any deaths. Just teach them a lesson, that's all."

His bodyguard nodded, understanding, and waited. A

few moments later there was the sound of a melodious hooter. This was followed by a billow of smoke and in its wake a couple of stones were hurled into the Eze's compound.

"There they go," roared all the bodyguard together, and went after them.

The sun, down in the West, had broken into fragments of purple when the chase started. The Mercedes led the race, closely accompanied by the tip-lorry. Then came the pursuing truck. This was followed after a long interval by the Volkswagen in which sat Kabu-Kabu and Onuma. Kabu-Kabu was going to see the Eze's order carried out, but the secretary took care not to be identified with the thugs in the truck.

The market at Isu was breaking up and people were going home, sauntering leisurely across the highway. There were frantic screams as the four vehicles mowed through their midst. The highway, after emerging from Isu, cut through a long stretch of low bush, and at this time of evening the green acres sloped in lush brilliance down to the bluish horizon. A little later the landscape was broken again by settlements, a stretch of thatch dwellings dotted here and there with white corrugated iron. This was the small self-contained hamlet of Mbamili now about to go to an early bed and apparently oblivious of the chase.

The Mercedes was way ahead, but the tip-lorry was making a gallant effort to keep up with it. Then, just at this stage, the vehicles had to climb a long steep hill. The Mercedes pulled ahead with Chief Ikpa. But the tip-lorry bearing his thugs laboured up more painfully.

The pursuers, aiming at their chief quarry, at first intended to overtake the tip-lorry, but a sudden taste for a practical joke caused the driver of the truck to pace the tip-lorry, shouldering it to the side. The thugs on both lorries leaned over the sides of their vehicles shaking their fists and hurling abuse at each other. They were primed up for a free-for-all if the drivers would only stop, but apparently the drivers had more sense.

The verbal fight continued until both lorries approached the crest of the hill where the precipice of Isu was. The tip-lorry was perilously close to the edge of the chasm. Then the truck lunged powerfully into it. There was frantic cries from Ikpa's men, the tip-lorry hesitated for a while, then plunged into the chasm.

The Eze's thugs gave a roar of triumph and hurtled on in pursuit of the run-away Mercedes. Two miles later, at Aniocha, they caught up with it, parked by the side of the road. Chief Ikpa had decided that his pursuers had given up the chase and was expressing his relief by making water behind his car. When he saw the truck bearing down on him he ran for the nearest house holding up his trousers as best he could. His driver, unencumbered, was way ahead of him.

The trousers saved Chief Ikpa. The first thug had jumped after him with a cutlass but something about Chief Ikpa's demeanour caused him to burst out laughing. The others were infected by his mood and were soon floundering with uncontrollable mirth. Even Gorilla who, with matchet in hand, had halted puzzled and frowning, suddenly relaxed and showed his teeth.

They could not get into the house to extract Chief Ikpa for even they respected the village code by which a refugee in a man's house was to be safe from molestation.

Gorilla went back to the truck, brought out a sprayer filled with petrol and sprayed it all over the luxury Mercedes. Then carefully, meticulously, he set fire to it. The thugs waited to see the big blaze, one or two did a war dance sequence, then they all got back into the truck and drove home singing.

Kabu-Kabu and Onuma had watched the incident from afar. As soon as Kabu-Kabu guessed what the thugs were about to do he dolefully directed Onuma to a hidden corner from which they could watch the proceedings. As the tongues of fire licked the Mercedes he patted his face doubtfully: "Not right at all, this is not what the Eze wanted," he said.

The two acts of violence raised a great stir, particularly the burning of the car. It is true that seven dead bodies were taken from the wrecked lorry, but the wreckage was referred to as an accident and after the lurid details had been splashed in the newspapers the incident was promptly forgotten. The burning of the car was not. Chief Ikpa worked hard to sustain the curiosity of the surrounding villages. And for weeks after the event the debris of the car became a centre of attraction for tourists. Then, as a result of repeated protests made to the government, a detachment of armed police was sent to Aniocha. For three days they paraded the market place, issued futile threats, and took statements from all sorts of unlikely people. In the end, in spite of Ikpa's accusations which he claimed he would substantiate, no arrests were made. But there was a statement from the commissioner of police read in the market places or broadcast by gong-strikers. It warned people against the use of violence. The Eze, too, in a release from his palace of Isu, pleaded that it was the dearest wish of the people of the ten towns that the forthcoming elections would be *free* and *fair*.

As a result of the raid Onuma found himself in possession of the Volkswagen car, perhaps for keeps. There was the likelihood, too, that at the end of election, given the right kind of goodwill, he might retain the car. It had frequently happened in the past that people who drove party cars forgot to return them.

One afternoon, just as he was settling to a beer at an Isu bar, Magic breezed in and was soon weaving in and out of the other customers. He caught the eye of Onuma, smiled his half smile and came over: "The Eze has done it again!" he whispered conspiratorially.

"What?" asked Onuma.

"The car that was burnt in Aniocha. You know he did it?"

"No," said Onuma.

Magic gave him a sharp look, wondering whether Onuma was lying. At last he decided that he was speaking the truth and seemed smugly satisfied to be ahead of Onuma in the firm grasp of local events.

"It was our big *oga* who worked it," he continued in low tones. "But he had to pay the police a fortune to get out of trouble."

Onuma's acquisition of a Volkswagen was also very much in Magic's thoughts. He did not refer to it directly but by allusions. For two weeks he said he had been learning to drive a car and he hoped one of these days the Party would reward his services.

Onuma offered him beer. Magic hesitated; he didn't drink but Onuma's offer might be a challenge which it would be unbecoming to decline. He accepted. Two beers later he was tipsy and began making sudden, violent passes at the waitresses.

Onuma judged it was time to leave. But Magic stuck to him. "Let us go up together," he said. And as they were stumbling out, he muttered tipsily: "You mean you don't go for that kind of thing?"

"Which thing?"

"The girls," Magic leered.

"No."

"Haw haw!"

When they got to the car, Magic begged to be allowed to drive and was so persistent that Onuma agreed to give him a trial. If after the first one hundred yards or so he proved incapable it would not be difficult to stop him and take over. But surprisingly Magic, in spite of his tipsiness, had full, competent control of the car. He drove faultlessly until they reached Aniocha, then with a triumphant gesture he stopped the car, got out and extended his hand genially to the villagers resting by the market. There were loud congratulatory shouts around him.

"Have you just carried this new job out?" somebody asked, pointing to the car.

Magic evaded the question but implied with his manner that he had something to do with the process of party car distribution.

"The Party is great you know. Vote for the NPU!"

"NPU!" shouted the peasants.

Magic came back to the car smiling triumphantly and drove off.

"The Eze will win. There is no doubt it," he said. "If I were that cousin of yours I would withdraw. The people are behind the Eze."

"Perhaps," said Onuma, impatient to take the car away from him.

They got to the Udemezue compound but Magic did not stop.

"We have reached home," Onuma reminded him.

"Yes, but son of our fathers, won't you let this new job make acquaintance with my compound?"

The car made acquaintance not only with Magic's compound, but with a number of his children who rushed out and formed a noisy horse-shoe around the car.

"Never mind, father will give you one," said Magic.

"One like this one?" asked one of the children.

"Never mind." He rushed them out of the way and waved Onuma permission to depart.

15

Chief Ikpa had sent two peremptory messages for Onuma to come and see him. But Onuma had been too busy with the Eze, and besides he knew what Ikpa wanted to talk about, didn't feel too easy about it and was anxious to avoid further encounters between them. But Ikpa persisted and finally sent for Onuma's mother. Oliaku stayed with her sister's family for a week and when she came back was glum for days. At last she decided to have it out with Onuma.

She came into his house and after a few moments of silence during which she seemed to be collecting her thoughts she burst out with unusual force.

"It is not right. It is not right that a man should desert his brother and team up with strangers!"

"Yes mother, but I have to earn my living. If Ikpa will employ me that will be a different matter, but he won't. Can I work for him on an empty stomach?"

She considered this aspect of the matter, decided that Onuma was right too, and turned against Ikpa.

"I can't understand why he has to stand against a big man like the Eze. When a masquerader sees another more powerful than himself he should have the sense to walk by the side."

But she ended with "It's their problem. . . . I don't

156

know anything about it. What I know is: Ikpa is your brother."

Onuma also felt a strong sense of betrayal but pushed it out of his mind.

That very same evening a thin hooter sounded in front of the Udemezue compound. Onuma went out to investigate and saw Ikpa sitting at the back of a Peugeot car. This must be his second car or he may have borrowed it. He was dressed in his regal robes and tinsel crown. Onuma expected Ikpa to be a little deflated from sitting in a smaller car than his mammoth Mercedes and as a result of his well-publicized low fortunes in the campaign.

But Ikpa seemed imbued as ever with his cosmic self-confidence. Losing a prized car had not made him collapse. This fact helped Onuma overcome some of the self-consciousness and guilt he felt at having been present at the burning of Ikpa's Mercedes. As Onuma rationalized it, Ikpa took a chance and lost and should be man enough to accept the results. As for the fact of Onuma participating in the action against Ikpa, if only the fellow would let him explain, he would make it clear that he was at the scene purely by accident. But Onuma refused to make his explanations at the point of the gun, as it were.

Ikpa did not look at Onuma as he approached but bawled out: "Where is Udemezue?"

"What do you want with him?" asked Onuma defensively.

"Where is he?"

"I don't know."

"Tell him that his son has perpetrated an *alu*. And I am going to charge him before the courts of our dead fathers tomorrow. You tell Udemezue that. You tell him that I came to his *obi* and that he hadn't the courtesy to stay in and offer me palm wine. Tell him that I am giving him a chance to come with me tomorrow to your mother's town and save his son from *alu*." And at the conclusion of this speech made in an even, dry voice Ikpa made a sign and his uniformed driver drove off.

Onuma wondered why, if Ikpa felt such animosity against him, he bothered to help him cleanse himself. But then Ikpa was such a traditionalist. He would be as much convinced that Onuma's supposed betrayal of a brother was a sin against the earth as of his duty to have it cleansed by a ceremony of propitiation. When Onuma got back in the house he discussed the matter with his mother. She took it to his father and suggested he should attend the ceremony.

"Why drag me into it?" Udemezue said. "I am not a member of your family."

"Will it be too much for you to go and see your brother-in-law once in a while?"

Udemezue snuffed thoughtfully for a while then concluded he wouldn't go. He didn't give any reason to Oliaku but within himself he had decided that he didn't want to be dragged into political wrangles. Besides the brother-in-law in whose house the projected settlement was to be effected was a worthless man he thought. He took care not to be home when Ikpa called the next day.

16

This could really be a good way of concluding the nightmare of my stay in Aniocha, thought Onuma. Ending with a simple old-fashioned ceremony. He and Ikpa were to perform the *igbandu* ceremony by which relatives and friends pledged allegiance to each other.

For a great many people, it had gone out of fashion. But for others like Ikpa it would still have force.

Onuma with his sense of estrangement from the whole pattern of life of the village, its lethargy, its sloth, its smug conservatism envied Ikpa his easy accommodation with quaint old customs. Ikpa had a prompt memory for all feast days and remembered always to send his uncle the prescribed gifts. There was of course an element of political back-scratching in this, but there was no doubt also that Ikpa was genuinely fond of his mother's people. In return they almost worshipped him. His hooter and regal flywhisk were objects of legend around the village. Onuma looked forward to going with him to study the methods by which he had won the hearts of these simple people. The prospect re-enforced the sense of well-being which he was feeling that evening. His decision to return to the city had driven from him the heavy burden of paralysis which the village always laid on him.

Political campaigning had become an exercise in blood-letting and Onuma's disgust had reached a stage where it could propel him to action. Fortunately a great deal of money had come his way in recent weeks and he could get to the city and set up properly.

"Uncle will rejoice tomorrow," said Onuma, as he sat in his mother's hut later in the evening.

"Rejoice is too weak a word," said Oliaku. Then, stopping midway in pounding yam, she made a face and mimicked the way her brother would thank Ikpa for his gifts the next day.

Onuma and small Philip burst out laughing. Oliaku was one of the best mimics he had ever known. But her dramatic gifts seldom showed through her placid exterior.

As Onuma watched her patiently going about her household chore he marvelled at the strange mystery of love, patience and forgiveness that was his mother. As he watched her it came back to him in the form of both dream and memory.

He dreamt again of that experience which was stamped clearest in his heart. He must have been just ten at that time. His father had caught the small-pox. Powerful as he was, he was treated just like they treated any other man who had the dread disease; they isolated him in the wilds. Some man who had been through the disease and was presumed immune had been instructed to carry food and drink to the sick man. But this fellow, either through carelessness or criminal design, had not gone to the wilds for three days. On the fourth day just past midnight they were awakened from sleep by a growl as if from a wild animal.

"Who is it?" shouted the mother. But the darkness was so intense that nothing could be seen.

But the mother already knew and burst into bitter weeping. It was the father. He hung outside there, nearly a ghost, and growled the most unjust imprecations against the mother. At last his voice faded back into the darkness. The mother lay completely crushed, but this lasted only for a short while. Then she rose and gathered all the food in the house, and braving the chance of catching the dread disease, walked to the wilds. She continued to take food to him until he completely recovered. Curiously enough, the experience didn't seem to have had any permanent effect on his mother. She remained the same with the neighbours, always willing to give the querulous women of the kindred her placid sympathy. But as for the father, the incident deepened his distrust and contempt for his *umunna*.

On his way back to his room Onuma had an impulse to say to his mother: "Thank you, thank you for your goodness and your inexhaustible love." Instead what he found himself saying was: "Mother pray for me."

"Pray for you?" She did not understand.

"Never mind, mother. May the day dawn."

"We are all in the hands of God," she said, praying after all.

17

Ikpa was a little nonplussed when he learnt that Udemezue was not going with them to the *igbandu*. But it was not going to put him off. All he said to Onuma and his mother was: "The Udemezue family will have so much to answer for when the day of reckoning comes. Get into the car both of you."

Onuma took the front seat beside the driver and Oliaku was seated happily beside her sister Adu, at the back. They had so much to talk about, and while Ikpa waved his regal fly-whisk at crowds which gathered to cheer him, the two women discussed the domestic problems of Adu's married daughter whose two children were just old enough to go to secondary school.

Mbamili was only a mile away. Just at the edge of the town their way turned off the highway into a rugged path which had been eaten away by the recent rains. Despite the driver's solicitous handling of the car it took tremendous knocks as it bumped up and down the numerous ridges. At last it groaned to rest beside a depressed-looking compound.

The driver, as if following a well-worked-out procedure, sounded the hooter.

"It is you!" roared Nweze, emerging from the compound.

"Where is our father?" asked Ikpa.

"He is coming out soon."

"No, let him stay in. We are coming to bow to him."

The driver had already with officious eagerness opened the doors of the car and the occupants emerged.

Ikpa led the way, flying his whisk and looking about for possible adherents. But the village looked curiously deserted. The home of the ancestors itself to which Ikpa and Onuma were directing their pilgrimage scarcely survived. The outer walls had all been reduced to a few inches of crumbled earth. Within, two small huts gazed out at an insecure world.

A Buddha-like figure, encased in masses of flesh, presided over a number of household gods. Nweze roared at him: "Father, your great son has come home."

The Buddha nodded silently at the visitors.

"Okike, greeting," said Adu.

Okike turned his large eyes on his two sisters.

From this manner of greeting one would think he was dumb. But this silence of his was entirely in character. From his youth he scarcely spoke more than a dozen words a day. He was the eldest surviving male member of the family from which came Oliaku and Adu. And from his spare, empty obi and crumbling outer walls it was easy to see that he was the kind of man whom any self-respecting person would despise.

But to everybody's surprise Ikpa seemed to conceive a certain amount of respect, even veneration, for him. It appeared that Ikpa in his search for deep roots had fastened on Okike. Having lost his father when he was young he seemed to use the older man as a substitute:

every time he passed through Mbamili he would come to pay his respects and give costly presents to the father of silence. There was something else that attached him to his uncle. Okike seemed deeply and completely possessed of the true spirit of the old rituals. When he pronounced the litany of any of them his memory was faultless and unstumbling. He was for Ikpa, then, the only surviving link with a religion which had anything meaningful to say to his experience. This was why Ikpa brought Onuma to him.

Before the gods and ancestors Onuma and Ikpa were to pledge love and loyalty to each other. Okike's bond would be the only one which Ikpa would accept as binding. Before the ceremony started Ikpa signalled to the driver, who nodded, went back to the car and from the boot dragged out a fat ram. Ikpa ceremoniously presented this to Okike.

"Welcome," roared Nweze, as it were doing the talking for his father.

Meanwhile a number of friends and relations were gathering in the *obi*, which was soon crowded. One or two of them sought to embrace Ikpa in the old boisterous manner that they had used with him before he became a chief. He kept them off by fanning his fly-whisk, and the peasants retired puzzled.

"Let's get on with the *igbandu*," said Ikpa. "Before our fathers, in the land of the spirits I accuse this boy of *alu*. . . . Yes. . . ." Ikpa dared anybody to contradict. "To work with the Eze's gang is *alu* . . . I have brought him here to be cleansed. And he is lucky that he has me to get him out of trouble. Father Okike, I bow to you." And Ikpa discarded his embroidered robes and whisk, handing them to the driver, and knelt down. The Buddha solemnly bound them together.

At the end of the ceremony, the peasants avidly fell

on the feast which followed. Two old men had been having a violent argument, the point at issue being which of Ikpa's ancestors was reincarnated in him.

"He is the very image of his grandfather," said the first old man. "Look at the shape of his eyes."

"There has been only one member of our family who has been as bright as he is, and that is his first uncle, Agu."

"But Agu hadn't died before this boy was born."

"He had," said Adu quietly. "It was exactly ten months after the death of Agu that he came."

Ikpa had donned his robes again and said he was leaving.

There was a general show of consternation.

"You can't," roared Nweze. "Listen. You are in the home of your father and there you will stay."

Ikpa ignored this. "Come along, women," he said. Then he took Onuma by the arm and started him out, as if now after the pledge Onuma belonged to him.

The two mothers went as far as the car, then Oliaku refused to go further.

"We can't leave just like that. It is too bad."

"There is nothing bad," said Ikpa entering the car.

"There is something bad, boy," said Oliaku.

"Yes, we can't go," said Adu.

"Very well, you women stay. I will send the driver to pick you up tomorrow." And with a burst of the hooter the car slid away.

After surviving the bush path again, the car was climbing back to the highway when a big Pontiac passed it going in the direction of Aniocha. Numerous hands were waving from inside. Ikpa waved back happily. The Pontiac had slowed down and was backing towards the Peugeot. It came abreast and from the recesses of its back seats the huge figure of the Eze heaved itself out.

"My knees are on the ground," greeted Ikpa, bowing elaborately.

"You rogue," said the Eze. "What are you doing near my home?"

They embraced happily, then Ikpa pointed negligently at Onuma.

"You know my brother?"

"Yes, I know him," smiled the Eze. "I know him very well. Shall we go back to my place. This calls for the hot drink."

"Thank you," said Ikpa. "We have work in hand. You know you stand no chance against me."

"I know," smiled the Eze grimly. Then with a wink: "Well, shall we celebrate after the election."

"Yes, that will be the time."

They shook hands vigorously, two successful men together.

18

The ceremony, as far as Onuma was concerned, had not been a success. He remembered being specially offended by the wobbly countenance of his uncle, by the peasant's unashamed rapacity. In between the drinking, he had gone into one of the outhouses to take coal-fire for a cigarette as his matches were finished. And he had seen one of those pathetic sights which are common in the villages: a brood of pot-bellied, naked, wet-looking children scrambling for a clay pot of sacrificial pottage. His aunt, a pock-marked, bed-bug ridden old woman, presided over them, shouting and cuffing the frenzied urchins. Onuma had hurried away from the sight without even taking the coal-fire.

If only one had the means of erasing such sights for ever. But how much would it take to feed the multitude of hungry mouths? And their brothers in other lands? Onuma was overwhelmed by a deep sense of helplessness. It was a consolation to know that he was soon to get away from it all.

The *igbandu* had been a failure for another reason; he had seen quite clearly that it had not been of much significance to Ikpa. Ikpa didn't believe in the *igbandu* but hoped Onuma did, and that thereby he would have a means of using him. Onuma was only a pawn in Ikpa's game with the Eze. Onuma hated the idea of being used. He hated much more the idea that through his passiveness he had been nothing but a pawn all these months, a tool for all kinds of combatants to use. Well it was all over now. He had seized his destiny in his own hands. He would begin to function again. But the Eze had been kind to him and he ought to clear up any misunderstanding between them. So he decided he would go to Isu the next day.

Later that night Magic came to see him and was wearing an important manner.

"Have you been to see the Eze?" he asked.

"No."

"He told me he would want to see you." Magic actually had been to Isu that day to collect bribe money for the elders of Aniocha. Remembering the role Onuma played on a previous occasion, he had left him out and gone with the albino. After the money had been distributed the Eze had casually asked Magic about his friend, the son of Udemezue Okudo.

"Why is he not with you?"

Magic, with a hesitant air, as if reluctant to tell on

166

a friend said: "Onuma? Well, he is gone with his cousin."

"Ikpa?"

"Yes."

"What does he do for him?"

"Well, I don't really know."

"Is he his agent?"

Magic smiled as if the answer to the question was too obvious. "The Eze must really have something big for you," he told Onuma afterwards.

19

Onuma arrived late in the evening, parked the Volkswagen in the forecourt and strode up, jingling the keys in his hand. At the head of the landing he met Kabu-Kabu and greeted him. This gentleman inclined his head mournfully. The inner sanctum of the Eze was guarded by Gorilla, who let him pass without a word.

The Eze welcomed him with unusual affability.

"So Ikpa is your cousin, brother?"

"Yes, he is."

"You want to leave us?"

"Well, not if you put it that way. You see—"

"You should leave. Ikpa is your brother."

"That doesn't worry me, of course but—"

"No. But you should go to your brother." He called out to Kabu-Kabu: "He is leaving us."

"But you don't understand. I like working here. It's only...."

"Yes, don't worry on our account," the Eze smiled. "We will find somebody to replace you." He turned away with a gesture of dismissal. Onuma got up smiling and strode out. Just before he got out of the door Kabu-Kabu held out his hand.

"What?" asked Onuma.

"The key," said Kabu-Kabu dolefully.

Onuma silently handed him the key of the Volks-wagen car.

As soon as he did so several hands came from all directions and seized him. His most vivid recollection afterwards was of the sub-human eyes of Gorilla glowing with blood-lust, boring into him.

After an eternity of pain he was dragged out and kicked down the broad steps.

He couldn't remember how he walked blindly all the five miles back to Aniocha.

He woke the next day his whole body smarting with bruises. He felt as if he had been cut into pieces and pepper rubbed into the wound. His impulse was to call for help but he knew nobody would be about. Only his mother had been to see him, when she brought his breakfast. A little dazed he had heard her drop the plate. Then there had been a pause during which she probably stared at him. Then, perhaps deciding he was drunk, she had left him and gone off. He opened his mouth to call her but the words would not come.

The words that came were a distracted version of the Christian admonition *Do unto others as you would want others to do to you*. Sometimes it was *Do unto you as you want others to do unto them* or *Do unto others before they did unto you*. The words danced about in his pain-crazed brain, somersaulted and then rearranged themselves like title-copy in a television commercial. *Do unto others before they do you*.

After a while, mercifully, his mind went blank.

When he came to, the pain had abated. And he was

conscious in himself of a singular clarity of perception such as is supposed to precede death.

The tenor of his life, especially over the recent months, stood out in sharp focus, all the stages through which he passed from a star of enormous charisma and energy to a futile disposable extra.

Viewing himself as if from the outside he saw a man who had long ago spent his emotional capital and was living on credit. Neither had he invested wisely in emotional bonds that could be turned into currency in a moment of need. Instead of investing in enduring values he had invested in transient ones. So when in crisis he sought a spiritual ballast it was not there.

The things that made him a personality – his essential honesty, his loyalty, his love for people, his compassion – had atrophied for lack of use. In his pursuit of ephemera he had discounted and neglected to cultivate human beings. There was progressively a gradual alienation until he had lost the knack of relating to them.

Also the paralysis of will which had overcome him at the latter end of his crisis of soul was symptomatic of bankruptcy of passion. For human action is in the final analysis the fruit of passion. Will is an accumulation of passion. When the passion is spent, then the will becomes diffuse and action is weak or impossible.

Very well then, he would re-order his priorities.

Find a different kind of idyll to love and care for. Begin again. And all will be well.

Onuma felt happy again as he contemplated a new life in Lagos. His flat and his possessions would still be available as a base from which to start a new life. Friday would have taken care of the place. . . . Friday was honest or just bone lazy. All will be well.

He sank into a calm, happy sleep. He was awakened

from this in the early hours of the evening by a sharp peremptory hoot which he knew by experience came from a Mercedes. A moment later he stood by the massive gate of the compound and saw indeed a Mercedes car. Magic was just getting out of it, waving brightly at Onuma, walking cheerily up to him.

"They told me about it," he said. "It was a terrible mistake. I have spoken to the Eze about you. He is a good man and I know he will take you back." His voice sank to a whisper. "If you want your job back you could find out what your cousin is doing. The Eze wants to know. I could carry the message to him." Then his voice resumed its cheery tone. "You will be all right. I am going back to Isu now but I will be back later in the evening." With a brisk wave of the hand he walked to the car and drove away.

Onuma returned and collapsed on his bed. *Do unto others before they do you.* His eyes strayed idly to the gun leaning across the wall. He rose slowly, took it up and played with the trigger.

The sun was beginning to fail and the night was bearing down formidably on the earth. Onuma took up the gun, strode out and sat on the trunk of a coconut tree which had been felled some weeks before, and brooded with his eyes fixed on the ground. *Do unto others.*

Many villagers passed and, seeing him holding the gun, stood for a while and wondered. Finally they would shrug their shoulders and go off musing. He had always been strange since he came back. But they were to remember the gun with dramatic vividness later. Udemezue came by too, noted the gun but said nothing and walked into the obi.

Only old Imedu was moved to comment. He was passing by the Udemezue house when he saw Onuma in this strange state. He stopped, pointed at the young man and intoned: "Son of *alu*, son of *alu*," before he doddered away again.

Magic drove back as he said he would, just towards the end of twilight. He stopped for a moment to shout to Onuma, "It's going well. Good luck." Onuma shouted back, "Come here!" Amazingly, Magic did. He was just about half way when Onuma pointed the rifle at him and fired. But because of his very bad aim he had to press the trigger six times before it had any effect on the irrepressible Magic.

The latter, with a look compounded of triumph and horror, crumpled. Onuma dashed to him and quickly retrieved the car keys, then ran to the car and got behind the wheel. Tentatively he tried the ignition. The engine responded.

An enormous, orgastic excitement coursed through Onuma's body, causing him goose pimples of pleasure. Mentally he savoured the flanks and pubic softness of this beautiful new mistress. Then he began to ride her and she moved with lovely art and sensuous obedience, moaning softly, giving him everything, denying him nothing. He rode on and on, forcing her through the most erotic paces, swinging her, bending her, licking her, swimming in her. Tears of joy and gratitude streamed down his face. He went on and on, directionless. He was not going to stop, ever.